Murder Is Homework

A Susan Wiles Schoolhouse Mystery

by

Diane Weiner

For information, email **Cozy Cat Press**, cozycatpress@aol.com or visit our website at: www.cozycatpress.com

COZY CAT
P R E S S

ISBN: 978-1-946063-32-8

Printed in the United States of America

Cover design by Paula Ellenberger
www.paulaellenberger.com

1 2 3 4 5 6 7 8 9 10

Dedication

This book is dedicated to the memory of Jupiter, my little, white Bichon. He was part of our family for 13 years and I spent many hours writing with him curled up beside me.

Acknowledgement:

Many thanks to Tim Robertson at C.O.B.R.A. Self-Defense Systems in Ft. Lauderdale, Florida, for teaching Susan how to protect herself!

Chapter 1

By the time she ran out of the car and into the police station, Susan Wiles could barely catch her breath. What a Christmas this was turning out to be!

"We're here to see my mother, Audrey Roberts...Audrey Stirling. She was just arrested for murdering her husband. We need to see her now," she demanded.

On any other day, the officer at the desk would know she was Detective Green's daughter, but being it was a holiday, a recently graduated rookie manned the desk.

"Calm down, madam. She's still being processed. Have a seat."

"Processed? Are you kidding me? Do you know who I am?"

Mike Wiles put his arms on his wife's shoulders. "What she's trying to say is..." He stopped mid-sentence, sighing with relief at the sight of his daughter running through the door of the Westbrook Police Station.

"Mom, let me handle this," said Detective Lynette Green. She'd followed her parents to the station when the call came, leaving her daughters behind with her husband, and a table full of Christmas desserts. Her brother, Evan, home on break from medical school, tagged behind her.

The rookie nervously shuffled a stack of papers. "I didn't realize..."

"You were just doing your job. Now, please bring my grandmother to my office."

"But she's..."

"Now!" In her thirties with her long blond hair and girl-next-door beauty, Lynette's commanding manner threw those who didn't know her off guard. She led her parents and brother into her office.

"Are Jonathan and Janet still at the house?" asked Susan. Her birth father, who'd just relocated from Atlanta to upstate New York, had joined them for the holiday and had brought along a date.

"He was going to drop Janet off, then come down. He thought Audrey might need a lawyer."

Evan said, "Poor Grandma. At her age, this stress could kill her. I thought she and Richard were flying back to Florida this morning?"

The officer brought an athletic-looking elderly woman wearing jeans, a rumpled sweatshirt, and silver handcuffs into the office.

"Officer, undo the cuffs," said Lynette. The rookie hesitated for a moment, then did as he was told. Lynette closed the door behind him.

Susan immediately started. "What the heck, Audrey? What on earth happened? Did you finally snap and kill that abusive son of a b..."

"Mom, let me handle this. You're too emotional right now." Grabbing a legal pad from her desk, Lynette turned to Audrey. "Tell me step by step what happened."

The pregnant silence was more than Susan could stand. Her birth mother had been nothing but trouble since the day she'd found her not long ago.

Audrey said, "Richard and I had a fight last night."

"What else is new?" said Susan. Lynette shushed her.

"I was so angry, I grabbed my purse and went to the little bed and breakfast down the road. I waited for him to call, but he never did. By this afternoon, I'd calmed down and went back to the hotel to work things out."

"Always a sucker," said Susan. "How many times did I tell you that man was good for nothing."

Mike squeezed her arm. "Let Audrey talk."

"When I went to our room, the door was unlocked and I saw..."

"Saw what, Audrey?"

"Susan, this is hard enough for me without you interjecting your disapproval. Richard was on the floor, blood all over, and a gun was lying next to him on the floor."

Evan handed Audrey a paper cup of water from the cooler in the corner. "Take a deep breath, Grandma. No one is rushing you."

"Before I knew it, the police were there. One of them slapped handcuffs on me and read me those Miranda rights like they do on *Law and Order*. They think I murdered Richard."

Tears fell down her cheeks. Susan wasn't fooled. Audrey was crying, but it looked like crocodile tears from where she was sitting. Was it a relief to finally be rid of that jerk? If she were in Audrey's shoes, that SOB would have been murdered long ago.

Susan jumped at the sound of a knock on the office door. Jonathan Stirling—Susan's birth father, Audrey's ex, and Richard's brother all rolled into one gentle, intelligent package, stood in the doorway.

"I thought you could use a lawyer, Audrey."

"You'd come out of retirement for me?"

"You're still family. And I know how hard this must be for Susan."

"For Susan? I'm the one sitting in a jail cell."

Evan offered Jonathan his seat. "Grandma, you should thank Jonathan. He doesn't have to do this, you know."

"I'm sorry. Yes, thank you, Jonathan. You're hired."

Lynette filled him in on what they'd learned so far. Jonathan took the legal pad from Lynette.

"What was the fight about?"

"The fight?"

"Yes, Audrey. You said you and Richard fought last night. Over what?"

Audrey looked at the floor. "I can't…"

"Tell him, Audrey," said Susan. "What are you waiting for? He's here to help."

"It was…he was…I'm too embarrassed to say."

"My mother, under arrest for murder, is afraid to say what she and her lover-boy were fighting about. Did you kill him?"

"Of course not! Last night, when Richard was in the shower, he got a text. His phone was on the dresser, and I happened to read it. It was from…it was from a woman."

"What did the text say?" said Jonathan.

"It said, *looking forward to more of the same. See you soon, Snookems*. I was shocked. After all, Richard and I are practically newlyweds."

Jonathan shook his head. "That's not good. Police call that motive."

"I know what a motive is, Jonathan. I didn't do it. They can't arrest me for reading a text, or for being jealous for that matter."

Lynette's phone rang on her desk. "Excuse me a minute. That's Jackson. He went to the crime scene. There are only two detectives in this town, and Audrey's my family. Let me see what he found out."

While Lynette spoke to her partner, Jonathan took down the details from Audrey. She'd confronted Richard when he came out of the shower, and World War III had erupted.

"He started screaming at me for reading the text. Then it got ugly. He said he needed fulfillment from a 'filly not yet put out to pasture.' I threw the clock radio at him. Then he pulled a lamp out of the wall and flung it at me. See here?" She pointed to a bandage on her forehead. "It bled really bad. I grabbed the keys and left. When I got back to the room the next day, he was dead."

"And you didn't talk to him or see him again until you found him dead?"

"No. I was angry, but I didn't kill him."

Lynette stepped back inside. "Audrey, this doesn't look good for you. The gun that shot him was registered in your name."

"That's because Richard was a convicted felon. He said we needed a gun for protection. I bought it for him, but it was all his."

"Your fingerprints were on the gun."

Audrey scratched her head. "There's an explanation. When we first got the gun, Richard made me learn how to shoot it. He took me to the firing range. That's the last time I touched it."

"One more thing. They found your blood at the crime scene."

"I told you we fought. He threw a lamp at me and I bled. See?" She again pointed to the bandage on her forehead. "Can I go home?"

"I'm afraid not. The judge is out of town till tomorrow. You'll have to spend the night here."

"But we'll have you out on bail tomorrow," said Jonathan. "Meanwhile, I'm sure it won't take long to find the real killer."

Susan said, "Didn't anyone at the hotel hear the gunshot? If Audrey had already left and someone heard the shot afterwards..."

"Jackson says the hotel was nearly deserted, being Christmas Eve. No one heard any gunshots."

Susan paced back and forth. "Richard had lots of enemies. He was in prison here for decades. I'm sure he kept some seedy contacts."

Mike said, "And he was involved in the drug business out at Agromex. Can't believe he got off. Not enough evidence. Bull. He should have been back in prison."

"And who is this mysterious *Snookems?* I bet she had something to do with it," added Evan.

The officer stepped back in. He looked at Lynette and in a shaky voice said, "I'm afraid we have to take her now."

"They'll take good care of you overnight," said Lynette. She shot the rookie a stern look.

"Think over the details," said Jonathan, "and make a list of anyone you think possibly could have murdered Richard."

Susan watched her birth mother exit in handcuffs. This *was* the worst Christmas ever.

Chapter 2

Susan slept fitfully. After coming home the previous night, she'd devoured the remainder of the Christmas cookies and gulped down the rest of the carton of eggnog. She still hadn't conquered stress eating, even now when it could be a matter of life and death. She got out of bed and checked her blood sugar. 208. Not good at all.

Mike was eating breakfast with Evan when she came downstairs to the kitchen. Her eyes fell on Evan, and she had a flash of him sitting at the table on his booster seat eating Cheerios. Where had the time gone?

"Sleep okay?" said Mike.

"Not at all. Glad you made coffee." She poured some into her 'Best Grandma' mug and topped off the cats' food bowls with Meow Mix. "Ludwig, Johann…breakfast."

"I made eggs. There's plenty," said Mike. "Lynette says the hearing isn't until 10:00 so we have some time. What do you think about Audrey's story now that you've slept on it?"

"What do you mean by that?" said Evan. "I hope you both believe her. Grandma could never commit murder."

Susan popped bread into the toaster. "I wouldn't blame her if she did kill him. Richard has been abusing and tormenting her since the day he got out of prison. I'm still questioning whether or not he was totally innocent in his wife's murder thirty years ago."

"You know he is. Remember, it was Jonathan and us who put those pieces together and got him released."

"I know. Still, I rue the day I got involved with that case. Anyhow, as I was saying, Audrey did have motive, and any jury would believe temporary insanity. I bet she'd get off without jail time."

"It's no guarantee," said Mike. "Besides, can you truly picture Audrey firing a gun?" He leaned over and pet Johann.

"And what about the other woman? And the prison contacts?"

"Evan, all those leads will be followed and hopefully the mystery will be solved quickly." Mike looked at Susan. "By the police!"

Susan ignored the comment. "Good thing Jonathan is living here now. I don't even know any defense attorneys here in Westbrook. Consider the options—our sleepy little town, or Manhattan, ninety minutes away? If I were a defense attorney, I know where I'd chose to practice." She helped herself to more eggs, and held some in her hand for Johann. She had rules about feeding the cats table scraps—only eggs, cheese, and the occasional empty ice cream bowl to lick.

Mike said, "Not to change the subject, but Jonathan and Janet sure seem to have hit it off."

Janet was the librarian at Westbrook High, where Susan volunteered. Slightly older than Susan, she'd become a widow several years ago and preferred not to retire to an empty house.

"I noticed that, too. Janet had her hair cut and she was wearing makeup. The sweater she had on looked new, too."

"I'm happy for them. I for one am all in favor of having a life partner to grow old with."

Susan gave him a swat. "Old? Speak for yourself."

She finished eating, then showered and changed. Not enough time to squeeze in her morning walk today. She made the bed and went back downstairs. It was almost time to leave. She puttered in the kitchen trying to work off her nervous energy. Audrey couldn't possibly be a murderer, could she?

When they arrived at the courthouse, Lynette was waiting for them. The lobby smelled like pine from the enormously tall Christmas tree just inside the door. The juxtaposition of the bright, colorfully decorated tree, the armed guard, and the metal detector gave her the shudders. *I hope when we go out back out the door, Audrey will be exiting with us. This is too serious. She'll die in prison if she gets convicted.*

She got into line behind Mike and Lynette. Evan brought up the rear. She was glad she'd cleaned out her purse the other day. Had she still been carrying the empty mint container, the knitted hat, and the red and green Hershey's Kisses foils, it would have taken much longer for the security guard to rummage through.

They followed Lynette into the courtroom and took a seat in the front row. Jonathan had arrived earlier and sat at the table with Audrey. Lynette had dropped off fresh clothes and a toothbrush for Audrey at the police station, but in spite of this, she appeared to have aged a decade overnight.

"All rise." It was just like on TV. Susan's legs shook. She couldn't imagine how nervous Audrey must be. The over-heated air in the courtroom tickled her throat, and she found herself working hard to stifle coughing.

The judge's bass voice broke the silence. "After considering the evidence, a criminal trial will be scheduled. The accused is to be remanded…"

Jonathan stood up. "Excuse me, your honor. Respectfully, may I point out that the accused is elderly and not a flight risk. We ask that she be released on bail while awaiting trial. Her daughter, Susan Wiles, is a long time resident of Westbrook and will make sure Ms. Stirling doesn't flee. And her granddaughter, Lynette Green is a detective right here in town."

The judge looked over at Audrey, pale and holding onto the table for support. The small Band-Aid which had covered the wound on Audrey's forehead yesterday had been replaced with a large patch of gauze, making the injury appear much more severe. Susan clenched Mike's hand and held her breath waiting for the judge's response.

"She'll wear an ankle monitor and be held on house arrest awaiting trial. Mr. and Mrs. Wiles, are you willing to have Ms. Stirling wait out the trial confined to your home?"

Susan's head buzzed. Did the judge say she had to live with Audrey? Maybe for months or longer? Couldn't she stay with Lynette and watch the girls while she and Jason were at work? *What are you thinking? Leave my granddaughters in the care of an accused murderer?* She felt nauseous at the thought of having Audrey around 24/7, but for lack of an alternative she took a deep breath and said, "Of course, your Honor."

After Audrey was fitted with the monitor, and a pile of paperwork was completed, Susan stood shoulder to shoulder with Audrey as they walked out the courtroom door. *Audrey won't be going to prison today, but will I wind up feeling like I'm in one?* Her relationship with Audrey had been anything but smooth in the time they'd know each other. Susan made up her mind then and there that this case would be solved quickly. She thoroughly trusted the Westbrook Police…but she'd do her part to move things along.

Chapter 3

Mike pulled the car around to the front of the courthouse. Evan helped his grandmother into the back seat next to him.

"Is anybody hungry?" asked Mike. It was early afternoon and Susan's stomach growled.

"I don't think I can eat anything," said Audrey. "Besides, I can't go anywhere with this noose around my ankle. Can we stop by the hotel and pick up my things on the way home?"

"I don't think that's possible. The room is still considered a crime scene. Tell you what. After we settle you in at home, Susan and I will run over to Walmart and pick up a few essentials. How's that sound?"

Evan chimed in. "I, for one, am starving. Why don't we pull through McDonald's on the way home?"

The ride home was silent. Evan held the McDonald's bag on his lap, snitching a warm fry and licking the salt off his hands. Audrey closed her eyes and rested her head on her grandson's shoulder. Susan ran through the changes she'd have to make with Audrey living at their house. More groceries, a full pot of coffee in the mornings...Was Audrey allowed to sit on the back porch with the monitor attached?

"Home, sweet home," said Mike. He pulled into the driveway and helped Audrey out of the car. Susan set plates on the table.

The greasy food hit the spot. Susan hadn't had fries in weeks. She looked at Mike, expecting disapproval—her type two diabetes was, after all, a big deal. Then she realized he, who had recently suffered a heart attack, was popping chicken nuggets into his mouth like a hungry Sea World dolphin scarfing down treats from its trainer. Audrey, who hadn't eaten since she'd been arrested, managed to gulp down a strawberry shake and half of a burger.

"Susan and Mike, I can't thank you enough for letting me stay with you."

"We really didn't have a choice. We…"

"What Mom means," said Evan, "is family always takes care of its own."

Mike agreed. "We certainly weren't going to let you sit in a jail cell if we could help it."

Susan held her tongue. After lunch, she settled her birth mother into Lynette's old room. She quickly changed the linens and put out fresh towels, then asked Audrey to make a list of essentials.

"I only have the clothes on my back," said Audrey.

"I hate to break it to you, but you could wear the same pair of pajamas for a month. It's not like you'll be out of the house," said Susan.

"Really? I feel awful enough. Do you have to rub it in my face?"

Mike stepped in. "We'll pick up a few sets of nice, cozy sweats. And socks. Lots of warm socks."

Mike grabbed the keys and he and Susan were off to Walmart. Although school was out on Christmas break, the traffic was heavier than it had been in the morning. Susan remembered that just yesterday, they were eating turkey and opening presents. It seemed as if weeks had passed.

"Day after Christmas. The stores are probably crowded with returns."

"You're lucky you have the whole week off before Janet expects you to volunteer at the media center. You're done helping Theresa at the charter school, right? I have to be back at the city permits office tomorrow. It'll be you, Audrey, and Evan all week."

"I committed to first semester with Theresa at the Charter School, but now she's got things under control. The media center at Westbrook High always needs an extra hand. And I promised Jonathan I'd help finish setting up his new house while I'm home. That'll keep me busy." *And away from Audrey.*

Mike pulled into Walmart and circled the lot a few times before finding a parking place. The line at the customer service desk snaked around to the front doors, and they had to search for a shopping cart. *Why are they still playing Christmas music?* Irritated, Susan led the way to women's clothing and picked through a pile of sweatshirts, already rummaged through by early shoppers.

"Is this what we want?" asked Mike. "What size?"

"Medium, I guess." She threw red, green, and baby blue tops into the cart. With some difficulty, Mike found the matching bottoms.

"She'll need underwear," said Susan. "It's too weird buying underwear for my birthmother."

"Better you than me. I'll go get her the socks I promised."

As Mike started down the next aisle, Susan said, "Wait. Isn't that Jordan Chadwick? What's he doing here? I thought he was arrested for dealing drugs out of Agrowmex?"

"The kid trying on ski jackets? Yeah, I think you're right."

Before Mike could object, Susan wheeled her cart over to Jordan.

"Merry Christmas, Jordan. I didn't expect to see you."

"You mean because I was arrested? Lucky me. I got out on a technicality."

A technicality? He was selling drugs to high school students, transporting them using Agromex trucks, and locked me inside a refrigerated tractor trailer where I almost froze to death. He's out in public and Audrey is on house arrest with a monitor locked around her ankle because she possibly stood up to her abusive husband? Calm down, Susan. Play nice.

"Must be hard facing the holidays without your parents this year. The teachers at the charter school still talk about how much they miss your mom. Did you sell the family home? What are you doing with yourself these days?" All she really wanted to know was who bumbled up the arrest. She certainly hoped that person was fired. Why hadn't Lynette mentioned this?

"I've moved back to the house for now. I've taken over as CEO of Agrowmex. It's keeping me busy. Going to take a ski trip at the end of the month. It's been a stressful year."

"Glad to hear you're handling things," said Mike. "Best of luck to you." He wheeled the cart away from Jordan, clearing his throat to get Susan to follow him.

When they were out of earshot, Susan said, "What if he and Richard were still in the drug business together? Or if Jordan wanted out and Richard was pressuring him to stay?"

"That's pure fiction. You don't have a shred of anything connecting the two. They were both incredibly lucky to avoid jail time. I doubt they'd have been so brazen as to push their luck. Besides, Jordan inherited Agrowmex and his parents' estate. He doesn't need to worry about a side business. Let's finish up and go home."

"Brazen was Richard's middle name. If he was pressuring Jordan to keep the business going…"

"You're determined to start a suspect list, even if it doesn't make sense. How many times do I have to tell you to…"

"I know. Leave it to the police."

"Exactly. Now, what size slippers do you think Audrey wears? These are half price."

Chapter 4

The next morning, Mike went to work, leaving Audrey, Susan, and Evan at the breakfast table. Evan was studying flash cards on his laptop while he ate.

"Evan, aren't you supposed to be on vacation?" asked Audrey.

"I start my neurology rotation as soon as I get back and I have to be prepared." Evan always reached for the stars. It wasn't enough that he was attending Wash U, one of the top medical schools in the country. His sights were set on a becoming a true leader in his chosen specialty, and that meant impressing all the doctors he worked with.

"You know, I see want-ads all the time in the Banyan Beach newspaper for orthopedic surgeons. Lots of us old folks down in Florida with worn out knees and hips. And spring training for baseball. You like baseball, right? I'm sure they need orthopedic doctors all the time. Then there's the Dolphins, the Panthers, college teams…not to mention all the golf that goes on. You'd never want for business in Florida."

Susan felt her blood pressure rising. "Evan has decided to go into radiology. New York and Boston have top notch residency programs. So does California, but you don't want to go clear across the country, right honey?"

"Truce," said Evan. "I'll see where I'm accepted and go from there. In any case, when I'm making a real salary, I'll fly out to see you both no matter where I wind up." He got up and foraged through the refrigerator, taking a swig of orange juice straight out of the carton like he did when he was a teenager.

"There's more oatmeal if you want some," said Susan. She was ready to get her eating back under control and figured a four-point Weight Watcher breakfast was a good start. Her blood sugar was down this morning, but still higher than ideal. She poured food in the cat bowls, but Johann tried to open the pantry door with his paw. Knowing it would be a losing battle, she popped open a can of Fancy Feast and added it to the meal.

Audrey picked at a piece of buttered toast. "I can barely eat, I'm so upset. We have to find Richard's real murderer."

Susan scooped out a bowl of oatmeal and set it in front of her mother "We will. Hey, did you call George? I was thinking about it last night. Does he know you were arrested and that Richard is dead? He deserves to know his mother won't be coming back home to Florida anytime soon."

"Last time I talked to him was Christmas Eve. He'll be so worried. Maybe I'd better not say anything."

Susan pulled her phone off the charger. "I'm going to call him right now, before he goes to work. He may be able to help being he's in law enforcement."

Evan looked up from behind his laptop. "He's with the DEA. I don't think he'll be much help. Now if you needed him to go after a drug supplier…"

"Been there, done that," said Susan. "He's family. He should be kept in the loop."

Susan called George's home number. "He must already be at work." Then she tried his cell number, which went straight to voicemail.

"He won't answer his cell if he's on a case."

"Then I'll try him at work."

"Maybe you shouldn't bother…"

She turned away from Audrey. "Hello, may I speak to George Roberts, please. Tell him it's his sister. Yes, it's a family emergency." She waited. "He's on vacation? Do you know where? Or when he'll be back? Yes, I'm his sister. It must have been a spur of the moment decision. Do you have a brother? Does he tell you every time he goes out of town? No, I don't want to leave a message."

Evan said, "He could be on an undercover case. Vacation is just his cover."

"No, he hasn't been doing undercover work for some time now. Since he hurt his back." Audrey picked at her cold oatmeal.

"Well, then do you have any idea where he is?" said Susan. "If he had vacation time, why didn't he come up here? We could have spent the holidays together."

"He'll be in touch soon enough," said Audrey.

Evan said, "He probably met a girl and took her to a beach resort in Mexico."

Both Audrey and Susan shook their heads and simultaneously answered, "Don't we wish." George had a history of making poor choices when it came to women.

"In that case," said Evan, "let's make a list of suspects. You mentioned prison contacts and the woman who was texting Richard."

Susan pulled a legal pad out of the drawer and started writing. "I think Jordan should be on the list also. They were involved in the Agromex drug smuggling scheme. Richard may have crossed Jordan in some way. Easy enough to picture Richard rubbing anyone the wrong way."

Audrey looked as though she was about to object, but didn't.

Guess I should watch my mouth. God will punish me for speaking badly about the dead. Although, I doubt

Richard is up there with God. She pictured him in a devil suit surrounded by burning flames.

"Grandma, did Richard mention any prison contacts in particular?"

"His cellmate, Bruce Feinstein, lives near here. I heard Richard talking to him on the phone a few times. I think they met for a beer one night when we first arrived."

Susan said, "Let me borrow that laptop, Evan." She googled Bruce Feinstein. After a few minutes, she said, "Hey, there's a Bruce Feinstein one town over in Redbridge. And here's a business ad—Feinstein Animal Grooming, the *Feinest* in the state. That was easy."

"Are you sure it's the same Bruce Feinstein?" said Audrey.

"There's only one listed in the area."

Susan pictured a tattooed prisoner with arms like Popeye the sailor combing out a French poodle. She laughed to herself and imagined bringing in her babies for a bath. She jotted down the address and shifted her eyes first to Ludwig, then to Johann—busy eating their expensive breakfast. *It would be a way in...* On second thought, she'd never subject her precious babies to being bathed by a murder suspect.

"Do you have a phone number?" asked Evan.

"Yes, and an address. Want to take a ride with me?"

"Mom, you don't have a dog."

"Any good pet parent checks out a grooming facility before booking an appointment. I'll pretend I have a pedigree Bichon at home."

"I wish I could come along," said Audrey.

"Why don't you write down everything you remember Richard saying to or about Bruce Feinstein. And think about this mysterious *Snookems.* See if you can remember anything Richard may have said to lead us to her identity. We have three possibilities to start with. Let's get started."

"I'll do what I can."

"Oh, and keep trying to reach George. We'll be back soon."

Chapter 5

A thin layer of snow remained on the ground. It was one of those rare Hudson Valley days, where the winter sky was blue rather than gray, and the sun was visible over the mountains. Susan followed the GPS to Redbridge with Evan beside her in the passenger seat.

"Evan, I wish you could stay longer. I hope you're seriously considering doing your residency here. Don't listen to Audrey. You'd be miserable dealing with those crotchety retirees down in Florida."

"Wherever I wind up, you'll still see me."

"How serious are things getting with that teacher you're dating? If I have more grandkids, I want to spend a lot of time with them just like I do with Annalise and Mia."

Evan pointed out the window. "Look. It's a billboard advertising, "Feinstein Pet Grooming, the *Feinest* in the state." See the picture of the thug holding the Shitzu? Looks like an ex-con, doesn't he?"

Susan couldn't concentrate on the road and the visual at the same time. "I'll take your word for it. Anyway, we'll see him in person soon enough."

She pulled onto a dirt driveway and followed it to an old farmhouse with an enclosed porch to the side. A hand-painted sign read 'pet gromming.' *Guess he didn't take advantage of those prison literacy classes our tax dollars are paying for.*

Evan followed her to the front door and rang the cowbell hanging from the overhang. Immediately they heard barking.

"Can I help you?" Bruce Feinstein was the size of a linebacker with tattooed arms and a goatee. His off-white canvas apron was covered in shampoo bubbles, making Susan wonder why he wasn't wearing one of those waterproof smocks like the shampoo lady at her hairdresser wore. His hands and forearms were protected by Playtex Living Gloves, at least one size too small.

"I was just rinsing a Maltipoo." He removed the gloves.

"We were driving by and saw your sign. I have a Bichon at home—such a bundle of joy. Evan here gave her to me for Christmas. Anyhow, I figure it's not too early to find Princess Kate a groomer. We call her Katie for short." She fingered the jeweled collars displayed on the front counter. *For the price he's charging, these better be real diamonds.*

"I do lots of those kinda dogs. Service includes shampoo, cut and style...I'll trim and even paint the toenails for you. Flea bath is extra." He handed her a flyer with the rates.

"Sounds good. I'll give you a call when we're ready for an appointment."

A burly man in a leather jacket came in carrying a dog in a crate. "Hey, Bruce. Can you get Rocky ready for tonight?" He looked at Susan and Evan, noticing them for the first time. "Uhh, Rocky needs a bath. My in-laws are coming over for dinner tonight."

Susan peeked into the crate, causing the dog to growl and bark. "Heavens, he must be a great watchdog. What breed is he?"

Without missing a beat, the man said, "American Bulldog."

"Well, I'm sure being nice and clean will impress the in-laws." The dog growled at Susan. "Let's go, Evan."

Once safely outside, Susan and Evan stopped in the driveway.

"Mom, you hear that mean-spirited barking? It's coming from the back of the house."

"That doesn't sound like a toy poodle to me. What sort of dog do you think it is?"

"Some kind of watch dog."

"People don't bring watch dogs for grooming, do they?"

"I thought as much when the guy came in with the American Bulldog. Maybe it's his own pet dog."

"Let's check it out." Susan led Evan to the porch, enclosed on the top with storm glass, and on the bottom with wood. She peeked in and the barking accelerated. "Evan, that dog has a muzzle on! Don't you find that strange?"

"Yeah, who takes a muzzled dog to a groomer? I'd hose him down in the backyard if it were my dog. Anyhow, let's go before Bruce wonders what's causing the commotion and sees us snooping."

Susan checked her phone once they were on the way, disappointed she didn't have a message from George. She didn't relish the thought of spending the afternoon in the house with Audrey.

"Evan, let's stop by Jonathan's and see how the unpacking is coming along. Want to grab lunch first?"

"Sure. Can we go to Vinny's? I'm in the mood for a meatball sub."

Vinny's was a family favorite—wood ovens, waitresses dressed in the colors of the Italian flag, and the smell of garlic permeating the entire place. Susan did some quick calculations. *A slice of pizza with a salad...thin crust...oil and vinegar dressing. I can keep it under 10 Weight Watcher points if I exercise a bit of self-control.* The rosy-cheeked owner greeted them at the door.

"Welcome. Don't usually get to see this pretty lady during lunch rush."

No wonder his business is thriving. He flirts with all the ladies in town, making us feel like queens. "Schools are closed so I'm taking advantage of the opportunity."

"You and your handsome lunch date. How's med school?"

"Lots of work, but I'm liking it."

Most of the tables were full. Susan noticed several college kids home for the holiday. She'd taught music to many of them when they came through Westbrook Elementary. *Time really does fly.*

Vinny led them to a table by the window. "Enjoy."

"This place never changes," said Evan.

"That's one of the reasons I like it," said Susan. She ordered the lunch special—a slice of pizza and a salad. Without opening the menu, Evan ordered the meatball sub.

"Mom, aren't you supposed to check your blood sugar?"

"Yes, Evan. I was just about to do that." She pulled the meter from her purse. "See. 110. Perfect." *Bad enough having Lynette hounding me all the time.*

Susan looked around the restaurant. "Hey, that's Stephanie, the receptionist from Westbrook Charter. Looks like she's with her mom—and a pet dog. Since when do they allow pets in restaurants?"

"I'll bet it's one of those therapy dogs."

"A poodle? And I thought therapy dogs were for blind people."

"Nah. It's the latest thing. It's not hard to register a pet as a therapy dog. People use them for depression, anxiety…you name it. And they get to fly free on airplanes. There were two on my flight from St. Louis."

Stephanie waved from her table and Susan went over to her.

"Susan, this is my Mom, Ellen. And that's her dog, Mara."

"Nice to meet you both." She looked at Ellen's wrist. "What a beautiful bracelet."

"Stephanie and I spent the morning over at the indoor flea market. Della Hops and her band of hippies were making and selling these, along with matching earrings and necklaces, see." She pushed back her hair to reveal beaded turquoise earrings. "You know how every winter they come indoors with their arts and crafts. Can't be growing tomatoes in the snow now, can you?"

"No, and with the competition from Agrowmex, I've noticed them selling woven purses and paintings at their road-side stands along with the produce."

Mara nudged Susan with her nose, and Susan stroked her fur. She noticed the Christmas bandana tied around Mara's neck. The dog was white as new snow and vaguely smelled of cologne.

"Ellen, where do you get Mara groomed? She looks so pretty."

"At Pampered Pups downtown." Ellen kissed her dog between its ears.

"Have you ever heard of Feinstein's Pet Grooming over in Redbridge?"

"Can't say I have. Can't imagine it doing any business, with Pampered Pups and Mona's Pet Salon right here in town. Every pet owner I know goes to one of those two. A few years ago, a third place opened and closed up a month later. There aren't enough dogs to support three grooming salons."

Susan pulled the flyer from her coat pocket and handed it to Ellen. Ellen put on the reading glasses which hung from a chain around her neck.

"Oh, my. This place charges double the ones in town. It won't last long."

The waitress brought lunch to the table. "Stephanie, Ellen, I'll let you eat. Nice to see you. And you too, Mara."

She returned to her table and told Evan what she'd learned.

"Mom, there's something fishy about Feinstein's, for sure. He's grooming guard dogs and keeps Cujo on his back porch. Stay away."

"What are you thinking?"

"You said the guy used to deal drugs? And he's an ex-con? He could be dealing out of the salon. I wouldn't be surprised judging by the client who came in with the *American Bulldog*. You know that's a euphemism for *Pitbull*."

"But Pitbulls are illegal here."

"Exactly. And American Bulldogs aren't."

"If he and Richard were working together before, then setting up shop alone would be more profitable. Richard had to be careful, since he was nearly caught. Not enough evidence, my foot. Maybe Richard was blackmailing this Bruce Feinstein and demanding a cut to keep quiet to the police."

"Anything's possible. It would take a bit of work to prove a connection like that. All you've got is a shady grooming salon, and a past connection between Bruce and Richard. You have nothing showing Richard and Bruce together after Richard was caught."

"Not yet."

The waitress brought the food to the table. While she ate, Susan racked her brain for ways to connect the two men. She was concentrating so hard, she forgot to open the dessert menu.

Chapter 6

Proud of herself for not overeating at lunch, Susan drove with her son to a subdivision called La Puebla. The development was new, built primarily to provide housing for the employees of Agrowmex, the foreign produce company that had recently come to town. This was the company Jordan Chadwick was now running since his parents had been murdered last fall.

Susan's birth father Jonathan's house was brick with white trim, on a corner lot. Bare, young trees dotted the front yard. The front door sported a large wreath, decorated with holly berries and a red bow.

"See," said Susan, pointing to the stoop, "I bought him that welcome mat when he moved in. And we got him the wreath when we got our Christmas tree."

"I know. I went to the lot with you and Dad right after Thanksgiving. You're getting senile, Mom. Better keep up the exercise and crossword puzzles."

Jonathan answered the door, wearing jeans and a sweatshirt. "Come on in. I want to show you something." Susan immediately smelled the rubber carpet backing, fresh wood, and coffee. She hoped Jonathan had found a lead in Audrey's case.

She and Evan followed Jonathan to the dining room table, where he had a bottle of jewelry cleaner and a magnifying glass. He picked up a silver ring.

Susan said, "Jonathan! I knew you and Janet would hit it off." *I love weddings!*

"No! This isn't for Janet. Heavens, we just started dating. I found this on my walk this morning, over by the river bank." He picked up the magnifying glass. "It looks like an engagement ring. See the inscription? *Say Yes, D.* And it looks like there's a date but I can't read it."

Susan started to take the ring, but Evan grabbed it first. Holding it to his eye, he said, "I see 9, 10, and a 70 something. Can't read the rest."

"Where did you find it, again?" said Susan.

"Down by the river, like I said. The developers are digging to build more lots down there. It must have been buried for who knows how long. Looks like an engagement ring, right?"

"An off-beat one. There's no diamond or anything, but with the inscription, I'd say it is."

"Imagine losing your engagement ring? I'm going to find the owner and return it."

"But Jonathan, by what we can see of the date, it looks like it was lost in the seventies. The owner may have moved away or even died by now. There used to be a park by the river, before all this construction started. When Mike and I were dating, we sometimes took a picnic lunch down there. There were cherry trees next to the picnic tables. We'd eat the cherries right off the tree."

"I've got time. I feel like I found it for a reason. Won't hurt to search. A park. Maybe that's where the guy proposed."

Susan said, "Such a heart. Let me know if I can help."

Evan walked through the house, never having been there. The living room had a brick fireplace with stacks of firewood next to it. The furniture was oversized and comfy looking. It opened into the dining room, where they now stood. "Is that the kitchen?"

"Yes. Coffee's on. Grab a mug."

Evan opened the fridge. "Almond milk, tofu, apples...Looks like your making healthy food choices."

"I try. There are Pop-Tarts in the cabinet." Jonathan cleared his throat. "For when Annalise and Mia visit."

Evan tore open the package and licked the pink frosting off before taking a bite. Jonathan showed him the rest of the house which consisted of a den, a spare bedroom, and a master bedroom with a marble bathroom.

"Nice place! Looks like you're pretty well unpacked, too."

"Need to get some artwork for the walls."

Susan said, "We should go by the indoor flea market one day. They have nice stuff, well priced."

Jonathan pulled a file folder from his desk. "I started working on Audrey's defense. Lynette has to stay clear. She says since it's a relative, she has to leave it to her partner."

"Jackson Simpson. He's married to a teacher, Theresa. I volunteered in her classroom at the charter school. Where do we start?"

"Audrey says she read a text on Richard's phone from someone called *Snookems* while he was in the shower. She confronted him, they fought, and Audrey took a cab to the bed and breakfast down the street. Then, God knows why, she went back to the hotel around noon the next day to apologize to him. She used her card key to open the door, and found him dead on the floor. Shot with the gun registered to her. She screamed. Hotel management came in and called the police."

"So we should start with finding out who if anyone visited Richard in the hotel that night. It was Christmas Eve. Let's go by and see who was working the desk."

"I'll get my coat."

They took Susan's car to the Holiday Inn. When they entered the lobby, a young man was working the desk. The hotel restaurant was off to the side, manned by a hostess in black and white standing behind a podium. The lobby was otherwise empty. Susan approached the desk, followed by Evan and Jonathan.

"Can I help you?" asked the young man.

Susan read his nametag. "Yes, Roger, is it? We could use your help. My mother and her husband were guests here. Richard and Audrey Stirling. Anyhow, Richard was murdered in his room and my poor mother has been accused of killing him."

"Oh, yes. I was working earlier that night. Couldn't believe it. A murder right here in our hotel."

"You have a mother, right? Could you ever imagine your mother as a murderer?"

"No, of course not."

"Me neither. In fact, I'd bet my life on it." She crossed her fingers behind her back. "We were wondering if there were any visitors that night? Did you see anything?"

"I'm not sure I should be talking to you. I told all this to the police."

"Yes, but this man here is her defense attorney. He has a right to the information and you know the police. They're not always willing to share."

Roger looked around the lobby, drumming his fingers on the desk. "I don't know."

"If it were your mother, wouldn't you want to know? It's perfectly legit to talk to the defense lawyer."

"Well, like I told the police, a big guy wearing a parka came in looking for Mr. Stirling just after I saw Mrs. Stirling storm out of the lobby. He used the desk phone to call up to the room. Then, Mr. Stirling came downstairs and they went into the restaurant. That's the last I saw. My shift ended and I was anxious to spent the last bit of Christmas Eve with my family."

"Can you describe the man?" said Jonathan.

"He was bundled up in a coat with a wool scarf half-covering his face. Like I said, he was a big guy—tall and stocky. Had a deep voice."

"Who came in to relieve you?"

"Petey did. Petey Johnson. He's the one who got me this job. He's working tonight."

"Thanks, Roger. You've been very helpful," said Susan. A suitcase-wielding couple requiring assistance approached the desk.

While Roger was occupied, Susan said, "He could be describing Bruce Feinstein. Why don't we have a bite to eat while we're here? Maybe the hostess or a waitress was working Christmas Eve."

The threesome wandered over to the restaurant where they were seated by the hostess. On the way to the table, Susan told the hostess, a woman around Susan's age with her hair in a tight bun, the story about her mother being accused of murder.

"By any chance, were you working the night of the murder?" asked Susan.

"Heard all about it, but no. I took a few days off to be with my kids over the holiday. Sorry I can't help you."

They had the restaurant to themselves, being it was the middle of the afternoon. A waitress rolled silverware at a table in the back. Another brought them menus. Susan asked both if they'd been on duty Christmas Eve, but neither had. Disappointed and not wanting to appear conspicuous, they ordered a light snack, ate quickly, and left. Once outside, they spotted the taxi stand.

"Audrey took a taxi to the bed and breakfast, right?" said Susan.

Jonathan immediately got her drift and approached a taxi driver standing outside his cab.

"Excuse me, sir. I'm a defense attorney investigating for my client. By any chance, did you work Christmas Eve?"

"Yeah, I was here. Good tips being a holiday and all." He took a puff from a cigarette.

Susan pulled out her phone and found a picture of Audrey. "Do you remember this woman?"

He scratched his head with his gloved, free hand. "Yep. Drove her to the bed and breakfast down the road. She was really upset, blubbering all over the back seat."

"What time was it?"

"I dunno. I guess around 11:00, the first time."

"The first time?" The threesome said in unison.

"Yeah. Guess she got a ride back here, then I took her to the B and B again in the middle of the night."

"The middle of the night? Not the next day?"

"Nope. Middle of the night."

"Was she still upset?" asked Jonathan.

"Naw. All business. Had a serious look on her face, no chit chat or anything. She gave me a big tip, since she'd forgotten to give me anything the first time." He snuffed out the cigarette on the side of the cab.

"Thank you, we appreciate the information," said Jonathan.

Back in the car, Susan said, "Audrey lied to us. She said she didn't go back to the hotel until the next day. Why would she do that unless..."

"Unless she's guilty," said Jonathan.

Chapter 7

"Audrey, where are you?" Susan slammed her keys on the hall table. "I need to talk to you." She tripped over Ludwig, as she stormed through the house.

Audrey came downstairs, dressed in a blue sweat suit. "What is it? I was taking a nap."

"Why did you lie to us? You killed Richard, didn't you? The cab driver from the hotel says he gave you a ride twice the night Richard died—once right after your fight with Richard, and then again in the middle of the night. You said you stayed at the bed and breakfast and didn't see Richard again till the next day."

"I'm not lying, I swear. I went to the B and B and didn't go back to the Holiday Inn until the next day. I don't understand why you're doubting me. You believe me, don't you Evan?"

Evan shrugged his shoulders. "The cab driver identified you. He was pretty certain."

A loud knock caused them to freeze. Susan answered the door. "Lynette. Wait till I tell you what I just found out."

Lynette took off her coat and tossed it on the couch. "I have some information to share also. You go first."

"Audrey left the Holiday Inn after her fight with Richard, but then she came back in the middle of the night to kill him."

"No way," said Audrey. "I'm telling the truth."

"The cab driver identified her," said Susan.

"What cab driver?" said Lynette. "Mom…"

"Jonathan, Evan, and I did a little investigating, since we know you aren't on the case. Poor Jackson is working all alone."

"Poor Jackson is in bed with the flu," said Lynette. "The cab driver says he saw Audrey in the middle of the night?"

"I showed him Audrey's picture on my phone."

Lynette sat on the couch and pulled a photocopy of a driver's license from her purse. "Have a look. I think I found Snookems. Jackson traced the phone calls from Richard's cell."

Susan and Evan looked at the copy. "She looks just like Audrey!"

"Yep. Probably who the cab driver saw that night. Her name is Carmella DeMaio. She lives here, owns a dress boutique downtown. And get this. She volunteers to teach literacy classes at the prison where Richard spent thirty years."

"Then you can interview her; or Jackson can."

"Jackson is laid up at home. We'll have to wait."

"But Lynette, she could be the killer."

"And she's not going anywhere. She doesn't know we know about her so she has no reason to run. Don't go snooping around there or she'll get spooked. We have to wait a few days till Jackson's better."

"See," said Audrey. "I told you it wasn't me. I guess Richard has a type."

Lynette said, "I've got to pick up the girls from daycare. Did you ever get a hold of George?"

"No, not yet," said Susan. "Kiss the girls for me."

"I sure will. See you soon, Audrey. I'll see you before you go back to school, Evan."

After she left, Susan began plotting. *Jackson's laid up, Lynette can't go near Snookems. There's only one dress boutique downtown. Carmella wouldn't ever associate me with Richard. I could use a new dress for my neighbor's daughter's wedding next month.*

"Susan, do you want me to cook dinner?"

"I was just going to make chicken and mashed potatoes. I'll bread the chicken and start the potatoes. You can do the peeling and mashing after I boil them. Mike will be home soon."

"I can't believe you doubted me, Susan. I'm no murderer."

"Sorry. It just seemed that way for a moment there."

Audrey and Susan prepared dinner while Evan studied. Susan was already feeling sad about Evan leaving in a few days. Next week he'd be back at med school, and she'd be back volunteering with Janet in the media center. The holidays had flown by this year. *What's Audrey going to do with herself alone here all day?* She heard Mike's key in the door.

"Hey, we're in here." She gave Mike a kiss. "Dinner's just about ready."

"Good, I'm starving. Did you go over to Jonathan's?"

"Yes. He has a second mystery he's working on. He found what he believes is an engagement ring down by the river near his house. It's dated 1970 something. He's determined to find the owner."

"That'll keep him busy, not that preparing for a trial won't. Hey, Audrey, are you going to help with that? You can do research from here on the computer."

"Great idea. I'll give him a call in the morning and get the details."

Over dinner, Susan told Mike about what the taxi driver told them and about Carmella DeMaio. "Carmella teaches literacy at the prison. We think that's where she met Richard."

"She probably knows Richard's cellmate, too," said Mike. "Can you pass the potatoes?"

"Why didn't I think of that. Of course, she knows Bruce Feinstein. "

Evan said, "You have to think of motive. You're guessing Bruce Feinstein is involved in drug trafficking and he saw Richard as a threat but so far you have no evidence."

"And I'll bet Richard was trying to break it off with this Carmella aka Snookems. She must have been angry. If the cab driver saw her the night of the murder, perhaps she went to see Richard, he broke things off, so she grabbed his gun out of the drawer and shot him." Audrey folded her arms and sat back.

Mike added, "Maybe Bruce and Carmella were in it together."

"I don't see a connection, but it's possible." Susan took another helping of baked chicken, forgoing seconds on the potatoes. *Tomorrow I'll pay Carmella a visit and maybe go back to Feinstein's Grooming to take another look. I can run by the hotel and show the cab driver Carmella's picture, too. The pieces are here. I just need to fit them together.*

Chapter 8

The next morning, Susan ate breakfast with Evan, then drove downtown to the dress shop where Carmella worked. Because it was early, she found a parking spot right in front of the boutique. *I'm here to buy a dress to wear to a wedding. I'm not snooping.* Bells over the door announced her arrival as she walked into the shop.

"Welcome. Can I help you find something in particular?"

Same build as Audrey, same hairstyle—though Carmella's hair is darker. They even have similar voices. "My neighbor's daughter is getting married and I'm looking for a dress to wear to the wedding."

"When is the wedding?"

"May."

"I'm happy to see you're starting early. I just hate when a customer comes in needing a dress for an imminent occasion. Too much pressure. Makes it harder to concentrate and so much more stressful. Shopping should be an enjoyable experience."

"Shopping is my favorite hobby," said Susan. She began rifling through a rack of dresses, disappointed with the winter colors and long sleeves.

As if she'd read her mind, Carmella said, "That's our sales rack. We're clearing out our holiday stock. The new spring dresses are in the back. With your light hair and blue eyes, I have some pastels that will look fabulous on you."

Susan went through the spring dresses, pulling out the ones she liked. She wished she could do sleeveless, but she was too self-conscious of her flabby arms. She'd bought a set of weights at Walmart before Thanksgiving with great intentions. In their original box, they were still sitting on top of her dresser.

"I'd like to try these," said Susan. She followed Carmella to the dressing rooms and pulled the curtain shut. *I love this blue one with the sequins.* She pulled it over her head and shimmied it over her bust and hips. Even unzipped it felt tight. Sucking in her stomach, she peeked in the mirror. *Maybe it comes in a bigger size.*

Next, she tried on a simple coral fit and flare. *This is more like it.* She tried, successfully, to sit down in it. *It even leaves room for dinner and wedding cake.*

"How are you doing in there?" asked Carmella.

Susan opened the curtain. "Fits nicely."

"There's a three-way mirror over here." Holding the dress up so she wouldn't trip on it, Susan came out of the room and twirled in front of the mirror.

"That looks beautiful on you."

Susan had to admit this dress was flattering. "I love the color. Do you mind if I snap a picture of me wearing it?" Carmella nodded, and Susan put her plan into action. She stood in front of the mirror and took a picture in such a way she also got a picture of Carmella standing behind her. "It's a little long."

"We do free alterations. I'll get the tape measure and pins."

"First let me try on the lilac, tea length. I may not need alterations."

Carmella unzipped the coral dress, and Susan went back into the fitting room. While she was changing, she heard the bells tingle and a deep voice broke the silence.

"Hey, Mel. Are we still meeting at the bookstore later? I'll bring the goods."

Susan had heard that voice before. She parted the curtain slightly and peeked out. Bruce Feinstein! *What's a dog groomer doing in a dress shop? And what loot is he talking about?* She pulled the curtain closed.

"Do you need help in there?" asked Carmella.

Now what? She was afraid Bruce might recognize her voice.

"Ma'am, I said do you need any help?"

Susan swallowed and tried her best to disguise her voice, without seeming overly obvious. She heard footsteps coming closer. Heavy footsteps. What if Bruce recognized her voice and was coming to confront her? *Confront me about what? For all he knows, my bichon is waiting in the car. I'm buying a dress is all.* Panic gone, she answered, "I'm fine."

Carmella turned her attention back to Bruce. "I'll be there. We're running out of time you know. Got to go into high gear these next couple of weeks."

"I'm up for it if you are. Later."

Susan heard the bells jingle once again as Bruce left.

"How's the lilac working out?" asked Carmella.

Getting wrapped up in listening to Bruce and Carmella's conversation, she hadn't even tried it on. "I'm going to go with the coral, but I'll stop by for alterations after I find shoes I like."

"You certainly have some time."

Susan thought about it. Five months till she'd actually be wearing the dress. "Yes, and by then, I may need you to take in the waist also."

She checked the picture she'd taken on her phone— the one with Carmella in the background. *Think I'll make another stop before I go home.* It was beginning to snow. She turned on the windshield wipers and drove across town to the Holiday Inn, hoping Audrey's taxi driver was working. On the way, Lynette called.

"Mom, where are you?"

"I bought a dress for Natalie's wedding. Wait till you see it."

"You bought a dress for a wedding that isn't happening until May? I'll bet the bride doesn't even have her dress yet. What are you really up to?"

"Okay. I was just trying to help, with Jackson sick and you not allowed to investigate. I went by the dress shop where Carmella DeMaio works."

"You did what?"

"I needed a dress anyway. Carmella looks so much like Audrey it's uncanny. Audrey swears she didn't go back to the hotel until the next day, after Richard was dead. I'm beginning to think the cab driver mistook Carmella for Audrey. Can you find out if Carmella has an alibi for that night?"

"I already have that penciled in for this afternoon. Jackson was going to do it."

"I thought you couldn't investigate?"

"It's not investigating. I'm just taking a statement."

"I'm going to stop by…"

"Mom, I gotta go. I have another call."

She wasn't hiding anything from Lynette. She had every intention of telling her the plan to go back and talk to the cab driver. Not her fault Lynette had to break off their talk so abruptly. The snow fell in big, crystal flakes. The weather called for several inches of snow and curling up with her cats and spending her last bit of time with Evan before he left sounded just perfect. First, she had work to do. Pulling in front of the Holiday Inn, she spotted the cab driver bundled up in a ski jacket, smoking in front of his cab.

"Excuse me, sir. We spoke the other day."

"Yeah, I remember. What do you want?" He took a drag from the cigarette and blew a ring of smoke right into Susan's nose.

Coughing, she said, "Can you take a look at this photo and tell me if it's possible this is the woman you picked up the second time on Christmas Eve?"

The cab driver enlarged the photo and said, "I don't think so. I'm pretty sure it was the other lady."

Susan scrolled back to Audrey's picture. "You mean this one?"

"Yeah. I told you the other day."

Susan scrolled back to Carmella's picture. "They look an awful lot alike. Same build, same hair. If they were bundled up in winter coats and hats it might be hard to tell them apart, right?"

He looked again. "I guess maybe."

"Thank you for your time. Have a pleasant day."

Driving home, the roads were getting slippery. At the traffic light, she noticed a black sedan behind her. *That car has been behind me since I left the shop.* She looked in the rearview mirror at the driver and saw a man with dark glasses and a wool hat covering his hair. His collar was pulled tightly around him as if he was disguising himself. *He has to be hot with the heater on inside the car.*

When the light turned green, she turned in the opposite direction of her home. Then, she made an abrupt right, and another left. The car was tailing her. She didn't want to speed up with the roads being icy, so she pulled into a drive-through bank and made an abrupt stop. At that point, the sedan sped off. *Who is following me and why? What are they trying to prevent me from finding?* She turned the car around and headed for home.

Chapter 9

Because she knew her family would admonish her for sleuthing, Susan decided not to mention having been followed. When she got back to the house, Jonathan's new car was parked in the driveway. Mike was still at work. Inside, Audrey and Jonathan were huddled over his laptop. Evan sat with Johann on his lap, drinking hot chocolate and watching a movie.

"Susan, look at this. Jonathan found jewelry catalogs online. The same two stores that are here now have been in business since the sixties."

"I know. I use the Mom and Pop one downtown. Walmart has a jewelry counter, and there's a chain jewelry store in the mall."

"But those are recent additions, right?" said Audrey.

"Neither was here back then," said Susan. "How do you know the ring was purchased here? You don't know that the owner was local."

Jonathan said, "I was reading about the park you mentioned—secluded, hidden away by the river."

"You're right," said Susan. "Only us locals knew about it. We always took visitors to the state park with the waterfall and the hiking trails."

"It's a hunch, that's all. The ring is unusual. We didn't find anything similar in either store's inventory."

"The Mom and Pop shop specializes in unique designs. Pop's an artist.

"Can we take a ride?" said Jonathan.

"The roads are slick. Let's go first thing in the morning," suggested Susan.

Susan prepared sandwiches and soup for lunch.

"Jonathan, imagine if you can reunite the man who bought the ring with his love."

Evan said, "Just because he lost the ring, doesn't mean the two never got married."

"He's right," said Jonathan. "If he loved her that much, losing a ring wouldn't have stopped him. Still, it'd be nice to return it. Seems like he put a lot of thought into designing it."

"I'll bet when the time comes, you'll do the same," said Susan. Jonathan looked puzzled. "You know, when...I mean *if* you and Janet get serious."

"Way too early to even discuss it," said Jonathan.

Susan made a second round of grilled cheese sandwiches and served more soup. Afterwards, Audrey asked to look at family photo albums. Susan had mentioned her stash of scrapbooking supplies, purchased when Susan first retired, and barely touched. Audrey needed something to fill her time.

Susan pulled a stack of albums off the bookshelf, brushing off the dust as she set them on the table. Audrey leafed through one. The pictures were mounted with little black corners and the pages had yellowed.

"Susan, is this you and Mike? You look so young!"

Susan looked over Audrey's shoulder. "Yes, that's right after we were married. We rented the downstairs of that big, wooden colonial. The owner was the teacher I student taught with."

Evan had another album. "Hey, is this you in high school, Mom?"

"Freshman year. Can you believe it?"

Evan flipped the pages. "I didn't know you were a hippie!"

"I wasn't. Tie-dye and peace signs were all the rage. If you want to see hippies, look at that. That's Della Hops, from the indoor flea market. Now she was a true hippie—still is. Her parents were super conservative. Della demonstrated against the Vietnam War. Word was things got bad at home and that's when she founded the commune on the farmland where Agrowmex now sits."

"Was Mike eligible for the draft?" asked Audrey.

"He was just young enough to avoid it."

"And luckily, I was too old," said Jonathan. "Awful thing, forcing our young men to fight a useless war."

They were so absorbed in the albums, no one noticed Mike coming in.

"Who's at war? Susan, you promised you and Audrey would call a cease fire."

"They're talking about the Vietnam War," said Evan. "If you'd been drafted, I may never have been born."

"A distinct possibility. My brother had friends who were sent over and never came back. He was in college at the time, so he was able to defer and never wound up going, thank God."

Jonathan's phone vibrated on the table. "It's Lynette. I'll take it in the other room."

"Did you have a good morning?" asked Mike.

"Yes. I found a dress for Natalie's wedding."

"Natalie's wedding? I thought that wasn't until the summer."

"May, actually. I got first crack at the spring inventory. You're home early."

"All the city offices closed early due to the weather. Snow's already stopping. I saw sanding trucks on my way home." He helped himself to a bowl of soup. Audrey and Evan were immersed in the albums.

Jonathan came back in. "That was Lynette. She interviewed Carmella DeMaio. Carmella has an alibi for the night Richard was murdered. She says she was at her daughter and son-in-law's. Her daughter cooked

Christmas Eve dinner, and later they all went to midnight mass. Back to the drawing board."

"Not necessarily. Of course, her daughter will vouch for her. That doesn't mean Carmella didn't slip out at some point."

"According to the timeline, she'd have been at church around the time of the murder. Lynette can find witnesses, I'm sure."

"Let's not cross Carmella off the list until we can verify the alibi. I have a hunch."

Chapter 10

"Evan, I made waffles." Susan fed the cats, then poured herself some coffee.

"Thanks, Mom. Soon it'll be back to cold cereal. Did Dad leave for work?"

"You just missed him." Johann jumped on her lap, attracted by the coffee cream. "I think I hear Audrey."

Coming into the kitchen in her robe and slippers, Audrey grabbed a plate and sat down at the table. "I'm starving. Scrapbooking takes a lot of energy. I couldn't sleep and it was a nice distraction. You know, I hope Lynette checks on Carmella's alibi."

"Of course, she will," said Susan. Audrey's comment just sank in. *How strenuous is scrapbooking?*

Evan poured syrup over his waffles. "What are you doing this morning?"

"I'm going to go back to my Weight Watcher's meeting. With New Year's coming up, next week the line will be out the door. Do you want to come and hang out at the bookstore? That's where the meeting is—they have a back room." *One last food fling tonight, and I'll be diligent starting tomorrow.* Her upcoming appointment with the endocrinologist, where he'd check her A1C, gave her additional incentive. *I'm pretty sure my average blood sugar will be better than last time.*

"Sure. Is Lynette coming over tonight?"

"Yes, the whole gang will be here to celebrate New Year's. Jonathan and Janet too. It's not like we could go out." She looked down at Audrey's ankle monitor.

Audrey said, "Don't let me stop you. If you have better plans..."

There she goes feeling sorry for herself. "No. There's no place I'd rather be than home with my family. Well, as long as a vacation in Tahiti is off the table. After my meeting, Evan can help me go grocery shopping. Any special requests?"

"You know what I haven't had in ages? Chex Party Mix."

"I'll pick up the ingredients. You can help me."

After breakfast Susan put on her heaviest jeans and a bulky sweater for today's baseline weigh-in. That way, even if she didn't lose this week, dressing in leggings and a t-shirt for the next one would give her the allusion she was back on track.

The driveway was a little icy, but the roads were clear, with snow drifts neatly stacked along the sides. They arrived at Barnes and Noble a little early, giving her a chance to browse. Christmas decorations and an electric menorah gave the store the air of seasonal festivity. A study group hogged the tables in the café. She wondered if the students ever actually bought books. She looked through the children's section, picking up a few sale books for Annalise.

"Hey, Mom. Look what I found." Evan carried an armful of books. "These are all about the Vietnam War."

"Have fun. It'll give you something to read while I'm in the meeting."

Susan made her way to the backroom. The meeting was sparsely attended, to be expected during holiday season. Susan paid for her missed weeks, winced when she saw the number on the scale, then found a seat in a metal folding chair.

"Susan, right? I'm Stephanie's mother. We met at Vinny's the other day." Her therapy dog was perched on her lap.

"Of course. Ellen, and your sweetie pie Mara." She scratched Mara between the ears. "Do you have big plans for New Year's Eve?"

"Just church and out for Chinese food with some friends. I'm starting this diet tomorrow."

"Church? On New Year's Eve?"

"Yes, I always go and thank God for giving us joy in the old year, and I pray for peace and happiness in the coming one. It's a tradition."

"Did you go to Midnight Mass by any chance? I heard the chorus was wonderful."

"Wouldn't miss it."

"You must know all the parishioners, right? I know this sounds strange. Thing is, my friend belongs to your church. Her Mom has been fighting cancer down in Florida and I haven't heard from her. I don't want to bother her in case, you know, her Mom passed. If I show you a photo, could you tell me if you remember seeing her at the service?"

"The church was packed, but I'll have a look."

Susan pulled out her phone and scrolled to Carmella's picture. "Here. That's her."

"No, I don't recognize her as a regular. I can't be sure if she was at midnight mass or not. She doesn't look at all familiar."

"Thanks for having a look. I'm going to go ahead and give her a call anyway."

The leader began the meeting by talking about enjoying holidays without overindulging. *A little late for that. She should have addressed it back in November.* Then she gave out a recipe for healthy oatmeal cookies. At that point, members began sharing their own favorite recipes. *I'm here to lose weight and all we do is discuss food. I could go for a* doughnut *about now.*

"Nice seeing you again, Susan. Next week? Same time, same place?"

"I'll be here. Have a good week."

She went back into the bookstore, hoping Evan hadn't gotten bored.

Just because Stephanie's mother didn't see Carmella at Midnight Mass, doesn't mean she wasn't there. I can't get my hopes up, but I have a feeling about this. There has to be another way to check her alibi.

She walked past the Romance section, then ducked behind the shelf. *I guess they had to postpone their meeting due to yesterday's weather.* She saw Carmella and Bruce, sitting at a table, nice and cozy next to each other. *I wonder what's going on? Bruce is out of prison, yet Carmella still sees him? Are they romantically involved? If so, perhaps Bruce was jealous when he found out Carmella was seeing Richard.*

"Mom."

Susan jumped. "Shh. That's Richard's cellmate and the woman he was cheating on Audrey with."

Bruce and Carmella stopped talking and scanned the store.

"I don't want them to see me. Let's go around the other way." Brushing past a table full of bargain books, she knocked a pile to the floor. Reacting to the thud of the books hitting the ground, she pulled Evan down behind the table. "Shh." Carmella, Bruce, and several other patrons, turned to look. She whispered to Evan, "Wait a few minutes."

An employee walked around the front of the table to restack the mess. Seeing her opportunity, Susan pulled Evan across the floor, and behind a tall case of e-readers. Hoping the coast was clear, she peered out from behind the case and saw that Carmella and Bruce had turned around and were once again engaged in serious conversation. Taking a breath at last, she said to Evan, "Come on."

Back in the car, Susan said, "Hope you weren't too bored waiting for me."

Evan gave her a look, then shook his head. "Not at all. The Vietnam War books were really interesting. All through high school and college, we barely touched on it."

"You were so wrapped up in math and science, you probably didn't pay attention to it."

"I was reading about draft dodgers and deserters. Did you know our town was a gateway to Canada?"

"I heard stories about men hitchhiking through here to escape the draft, but I don't know how accurate they were. You know how a little nugget of truth can turn into a full blown tall tale. People like to romanticize wars and look for hero stories."

"Yeah. I guess it distracts them from the gruesomeness."

She wondered how Evan would have any idea what it was like to be in a war. Luckily, his experience had been limited to what he'd seen in books and movies. She couldn't imagine having a son drafted. *Those poor mothers must have laid awake night after night, consumed with worry.*

Susan pulled into Shoprite, and circled around and around trying to find a parking spot. With the threat of a storm, they were closing early today. Finally, she found a spot at the far end of the grocery store. Making lemonade out of lemons, she pushed up her coat sleeve and glanced at her Fitbit. She had forgotten her grocery list, and distracted trying to remember what she needed, nearly collided with a tall man in a parka, pushing a cart of groceries to his car.

"Evan, I'd forgotten what the desk clerk said about the night Richard was killed. He said a tall stocky man in a parka came in shortly after Audrey stormed off. I'm assuming that was Bruce. I wonder if Jackson talked to him. That puts both Carmella and Bruce at the Holiday Inn that night."

"You don't know Carmella was there. Doesn't she have an alibi?"

"Not if the cab driver mistook her for Audrey. Her alibi was attending church and spending the evening with her daughter. If anyone would lie about an alibi, it'd be a family member."

"Yeah. Who wants to see their mother locked in jail, right?" said Evan. He grabbed a grocery wagon.

The store was so crowded it was hard to get through the aisles. Susan picked up a bottle of champagne, then sought out the ingredients for Chex Party Mix, grateful for the recipe on the back of the cereal box. In the aisle, she saw Theresa, Jackson's wife, with baby Ian in the front seat of the wagon, grabbing items off the shelf.

"Ian, no. Put that back," said Theresa. When she bent down to pick up the boxes Ian had dropped, he grabbed onto her dark curls.

"Need some help?"

"Susan! I was so distracted by Ian I didn't see you. Hi, Evan. Glad you were able to spend some time at home. Made your Mom very happy."

Evan picked up the other boxes from the floor.

Susan said, "Is Jackson feeling any better?"

"Somewhat. He's already getting a little stir crazy. I heard him setting up an interview on the phone. Remember Jordan Chadwick? He just took over as CEO of Agrowmex."

"Yes. Jackson thinks he may be involved in Richard's murder?"

"Oh, I don't know. I think he's suspicious Jordan has restarted the drug business, and Richard was involved also, so..."

"So if something went wrong, Jordan had motive to kill Richard."

"Something like that. I try to stay out of Jackson's police business."

"If Jackson feels up to it, and you think he's no longer contagious, why don't you all stop by tonight for New Year's Eve?"

"Sounds like fun. As long as Jackson's up to it, we'll be there."

Chapter 11

Susan carried a bowl of Chex Mix into the living room, while Audrey cut up vegetables and cubes of cheese. The heavenly aroma of cookies baking in the oven permeated the whole house. They'd finally been able to take Audrey's suitcase from the bed and breakfast and instead of looking frumpy in her Walmart sweats, Audrey looked elegant in a silky white shirt and wide black pants which hid the ankle monitor.

"Evan, can you get the door?" said Susan.

Lynette, holding Mia, and Jason holding Annalise's hand, came in with a bottle of sparkling apple cider and a pan of cheesecake brownies. Annalise ran to Mike.

"Grampa, pick me up," said Annalise. Mike held her high over his head and kissed her stomach.

"Annalise, you have the greatest laugh ever," said Mike. "Think you'll make it to midnight?"

"Let's hope not," said Jason. "Otherwise she'll be a cranky mess tomorrow."

"Mom, that cashmere sweater looks good on you. I'm glad it fit."

"I love it. I've already worn it three times since you gave it to me on Christmas."

She took Mia from Lynette. "How's my beautiful girl! I set up the Pack'n'Play for you and I added a few new toys."

Audrey carried in the rest of the food, and Evan brought in a few folding chairs. Soon, Theresa, Jackson, and baby Ian arrived. Before the front door closed, Jonathan and Janet pulled into the driveway.

"Come on in, it's freezing out there." Susan took their coats. "There's plenty of food, help yourselves. Theresa, you can stick Ian in the Pack'n'Play with Mia if you'd like."

Ian clung to Theresa like a baby monkey. "Maybe after he feels more comfortable."

Jonathan sat on the couch and put his arm around Janet. *Looks like their relationship is progressing nicely.* After losing their prospective spouses, neither Jonathan nor Janet had ventured back into the dating game—until now. *They make such a cute couple.*

Jonathan said, "I went over to those jewelry stores you mentioned, Susan. The owner of the Mom and Pop shop says it looks like the ring was made in the late sixties or early seventies. He recognized it as his son's work. They don't keep records that far back. His son is on a cruise with his wife this week. I can try talking to him when he returns."

Susan felt arms hugging her leg. "Grandma, I left my new baby that Santa got me in Daddy's car. She has to have her bottle. Can we go get her? Pleeeze?"

Jason was playing a video game with Evan, and Lynette was heating up Mia's bottle in the kitchen.

"I'll get it, honey. You wait here. It's cold out."

"Don't forget her blankie."

"I won't." Susan put on her coat, grabbed Jason's keys, and ventured into the freezing night air. She could see her breath in front of her, but not much else. Susan had signed a petition to get street lights, but nothing ever came of it. She made her way to Jason and Lynette's car which was parked on the street past the driveway. She stopped in her tracks. *What's that noise?* She felt a shiver crawl up her back. "Hello. Is someone out here?"

Too many scary TV shows. I should stick to the Hallmark Channel. She started toward the car again, then froze. She was sure she heard the snow crunching as if someone was walking on it. The icy wind stung her face. *Less James Patterson, more Cozy Cat Press. It's just your imagination.*

When she reached the car, she opened the back door and grabbed Annalise's new doll. She'd bought it for her granddaughter months ago when the new Christmas toys hit the shelves, but had wrapped it up and written 'from Santa' on it. She closed the car door and headed back to the house. Without her gloves and hat, she could barely stand the cold.

She was halfway back to the house when she realized she'd forgotten the doll's blankie. She whipped around. *Who's that?* She caught a glimpse of a figure running down the street. He was too far away to get a good look, but she noted that he ran swiftly and gracefully, like the cheetah she'd seen at the zoo with Annalise last summer. The hair on her neck prickled. *Let me get the darn blankie and get back inside.*

She opened the car door a second time and felt around for the blanket. *Got it!* In her haste, she dropped it into the snow. When she bent down to pick it up, she saw something. *Hey, what's this?* She picked up a large button. *This looks like it came off a man's coat. The thread is still attached.* She felt her heart thumping. *Everyone here tonight had on a zippered jacket. Who was here and what is it they want?* Returning to her original sense of urgency, she ran through the yard, trying not to slip.

When she finally got back inside, she'd almost forgotten why she'd gone out.

"Grandma, you got my baby. She's cold. Let me have her blankie."

"You hold her tight and she'll warm right up. That's it. You're a great Mommy, sweetheart. See, she's nice and toasty now."

Lynette was feeding Mia. "Thanks, Mom. Are you okay? You look like you saw a ghost."

"I'll be fine once I warm up. Where's Jackson?"

"We got a call from the station. A high school kid was brought into the emergency room. It was a Fentanyl overdose. Remember that drug? It's the one Jordan Chadwick was smuggling through Agrowmex."

"The Heroine on steroids. Evan filled me in. Do you have to leave?"

"No, Jackson can handle it over the phone for now. I thought we were done with Fentanyl. This is the first overdose we've had since Richard and Jordan were arrested."

"And neither stayed in prison. Jordan's probably back to his old tricks."

"We've had our eyes on him, but so far nothing suspicious. Taking over his father's business is a huge undertaking. We didn't think he had time to mess around with drug dealing. Anyway, we're putting the cart before the horse."

Mike said, "Enough talk about drugs and Jordan Chadwick." He took the Pictionary game off the shelf.

Every time they played, Susan laughed so hard her stomach hurt. Tonight was no exception. Janet and Jonathan teamed up and dominated the evening. The bowl of Chex Mix was empty, as was the plate of cheesecake brownies. Susan went into the kitchen to replace the food.

What was that? Looking out the kitchen window, she thought for a moment she'd heard the wind chimes. *I was outside earlier, and the air was as still as ever.* She pulled the curtains farther apart and flicked on the outside light. *No one's there. You have to give your imagination a rest.*

She heard Evan call from the living room. "Hey, it's almost midnight. Turn on the TV. Come on. Mom."

All three children had fallen asleep. Mike poured champagne while the crystal ball dropped and Ryan Seacrest led the countdown. *Five, four three two... 'May old acquaintance be forgot...'*

"Happy New Years!" Mike kissed Susan, Jason grabbed Lynette, and Jonathan and Janet smooched so long it was almost embarrassing. Trying not to stare, Susan grabbed Evan. "You get a kiss on the cheek from Mom. Maybe next year..."

"Next year I'll be lucky if I make it home for Christmas. I'll be doing away rotations and who knows where I'll be."

"Even if you're on call in Timbuktu, we'll be there in spirit. And on Skype."

When everyone left, Susan stacked dishes in the sink. Suddenly she remembered the button. She grabbed a baggie and took it out of her coat pocket. She wasn't wearing gloves when she'd found it, but she didn't want to add more fingerprints. *Maybe they'll get a partial. I'll bring it to the station tomorrow. I hope I'm not overreacting.* She knew from experience she wasn't. Somehow this button was tied into Richard's murder. She just had to figure out how.

Chapter 12

Back to the routine. Evan had returned to St. Louis, the storefronts of downtown Westbrook looked naked sans holiday decorations, and diet and gym ads cluttered the media. Susan had replaced the expiring carton of eggnog and the half eaten tin of Danish butter cookies with a pitcher of fruit-infused water and a freezer full of Lean Cuisines.

The aroma of fresh coffee tantalized her nose as Susan made her way into the kitchen, weighing the pros and cons of eggs versus hot oatmeal.

"Audrey, what are you doing up so early?"

"I couldn't sleep. I'm feeling blue now that the holidays are over and I'll be spending so much time alone with my thoughts. You're going back to volunteer at school, and Evan's gone."

Audrey half-heartedly worked on the crossword puzzle from the newspaper, which irritated Susan, since working on the single copy of the puzzle was part of her own morning routine. She took a few deep breaths to avoid snapping at her birth mother. *I promised Janet I'd be at school to help before the students arrived. I'll address this issue tomorrow.*

"Can we move up the trial? I really want it to be over." Johann jumped up on Audrey's lap, drawn by the cream in her coffee mug.

"Me too, but we're all doing our best to put together a defense for you. You don't want to go into that courtroom until we're sure you'll come out the door a free woman." The irony pained her. As much as she wanted Audrey out of her house, she didn't want to see her locked in a prison cell for the rest of her life. Prompted by soft meows, she poured cat food into the bowls on the floor.

"You're right. I told George how supportive you're all being."

"You spoke to George? Why didn't you tell me?"

"I got an email last night. He's been out of the country. Something about a rainforest getaway and no internet. He's on his way back to Florida."

"You told him what's going on, right? Why isn't he flying here to be with you?"

"He only has so much vacation time. He says he's confident everything will turn out okay."

"That doesn't sound like the George I know. He isn't one to sit by and watch." She made a mental note to call him later.

"I'm glad he isn't overreacting. Back in Florida he was like a hawk watching that Richard didn't hurt me. He was always trying to convince me to divorce Richard."

"Sounds like he was trying to protect you. Have to admit you should have listened to him." She gathered her things and set off to volunteer.

The atmosphere at Westbrook High was much different than that of Westbrook Charter. While she enjoyed talking to the older students, her heart was still with the babies at the elementary level where she'd spent the bulk of her career. *When Annalise gets to kindergarten, I'll go back to Westbrook Elementary.* She pulled into the parking lot next to the bus loop.

The office of Westbrook High was buzzing with new year greetings and vacation stories. After socializing in the mailroom, Susan made her way up to the media center. It was almost eerie—not a book off the shelves;

not a student in sight. Janet came out of her office and gave her a welcoming hug.

"Susan, did Evan get off okay?" Janet was wearing the new red sweater she'd helped Jonathan pick out for her Christmas present.

"Yes, he's back and ready to take on his neurology rotation. I miss him already."

"How's the investigation going? Jonathan seems a bit frustrated."

"It was a little slow during Christmas break. So far, we know that Bruce Feinstein and Carmella DeMaio both visited Richard the night he was murdered. Carmella had Richard's number in her contacts, and the taxi driver gave her a ride to the hotel."

"Didn't you say he identified Audrey as the woman in the taxi?"

"At first, but when I realized how similar Audrey and Carmella look, I went back and showed him Carmella's picture. He says it *could* have been Carmella he drove to the hotel."

"Jonathan said she had an alibi."

"She claims to have been at midnight mass, but so far no one at the church can vouch for the fact that she was there, only her own daughter and son-in-law. And, Carmella knows Bruce Feinstein. Chances are she met him at the prison where she met Richard. I saw them together at the dress shop where Carmella works and later at the bookstore sitting shoulder to shoulder like a pair of lovebirds."

A stocky, middle-aged man came into the media center carrying a list. "Which of you is the librarian?" Susan tried to read the volunteer badge around his neck, but it was turned backwards.

"That would be me. Can I help you?"

"Yeah. I'm the interim sub for the shop teacher. Duke. Duke Holliday. Do you have some sort of videos I can use?"

"For shop class?"

"Yeah. Or books or something?"

"It's typically a hands-on class," said Janet, noticing his bandaged hand, "but it looks like you're a bit handicapped."

"Stupid dog bit me. Shoulda put a muzzle on him. Hope it was worth it. Trying to pet him, I mean."

Janet led him to a shelf full of videos and DVD's. "Let's see, here's one on the art of woodworking. Here's one on flipping houses. Is that close enough?"

"These'll work. Thanks. Looks like you have some other customers." Duke exited, letting the door swing behind him.

Two girls made a beeline for the computers, while the boy with them stopped to greet Janet. Susan recognized the boy. Tall and clean-cut, he was president of the senior class and a star on the track team. She vaguely remembered teaching him music when he was in elementary school. *What was his name again? Charlie? Carl?*

"Chad, I hope you had a wonderful break," said Janet.

"Sure did. Waiting to find out where I've been accepted for next year. It's smooth sailing now. Hey, what's that about?"

Sirens blared from outside. Holding her sensitive ears, Susan made her way to the window just in time to see two of Lynette's colleagues jump out and handcuff a student. After getting the student into the police van labeled *canine* unit, the officers released a German Shepherd from the back.

Janet and Chad now peered through the window as well. "He's taking the dog inside. That means they're searching for drugs. Happened last fall right after school started too. Chad, do you remember?"

"Yes. We were on lockdown and they found drugs in one of the PE lockers. One of the kids involved was over eighteen and is doing time. The other two, I don't know. Haven't seen them since."

Susan wasn't surprised by the arrest last fall, but now? Lynette was sure they'd stopped the Fentanyl ring when they caught Richard and Jordan Chadwick. Had Bruce Feinstein taken over, running the drugs through his grooming shop? Or was Jordan Chadwick back to his old tricks?

Over the intercom, a 'Code Black' was announced.

"Oh, no," said Janet. "That means we're locked in until they give us the all clear. Last time it took hours."

Someone banged on the media center door.

"It might be a student. I'll pull him in," said Janet. When she opened the door, Duke Holliday, still carrying his DVD's, rushed in.

"What's going on? Not a bomb scare, I hope. Figures. They'll lock us in while they search. Makes no sense." He placed the DVDs down on the table.

Janet said, "They're searching for drugs. They brought in the canine unit."

"Hope they got muzzles on them dogs."

"We might as well make ourselves comfortable. This could take a while," said Janet, slumping into a wooden chair. "I have my little coffee maker going in my office if anyone wants some."

"Bomb scare, canine units in the halls...it was a different world when I started teaching," said Susan.

The two girls who'd been using the computers joined the others at the table.

Susan said, "So you're still having drug issues here at school?"

One of the girls sighed. "Yes, two of my classmates landed in the emergency room right before Christmas. They were at some drug-pumped holiday party at another kid's house and both wound up overdosing. It was touch and go. We heard they almost died. So stupid. If they were stupid enough to try drugs, they deserve what they got."

"I remember those days," said Duke. "Young and stupid. You think you're invincible, then wham. Life knocks you down."

Janet said, "The EMT's started carrying some sort of drug that reverses the effects of heroine. That's what saved them."

Susan tried to call Mike, but the internet was down, or blocked. She wondered if the police could cause that to happen. Hopefully this would be over before word got out and Mike got worried.

Bam. A huge crash. The lights went out.

"What's happening?" cried one of the girls. She grabbed Susan's arm.

Another crash, and Susan swore she heard footsteps. Then an alarm sounded.

"Someone opened the emergency exit. We weren't alone." Janet gasped.

"Janet, was the media center empty when you got in?"

"I thought it was. This is creepy. Where are the police?"

"I can't see nothing," said Duke. He started toward the window.

"No!" yelled Susan. Get down and don't make yourself a target. We have no idea who's out there. This could be more than a simple drug bust."

More crashing—this time from the hallway. The lights were still out.

"I'm scared," said one of the girls. Her friend concurred., "Me, too!"

"Shush! Stay still in case it's an active shooter," whispered Janet. The students seemed to know what to do. *What a sad world when school kids have to practice for such a scenario.*

Then as suddenly as they'd gone out, the lights were back. More sirens sounded from outside. They huddled together at the table for what seemed like an eternity.

"What's happening?" asked Chad.

"Do you think the school will close for the day?"

Janet assured them that this was all done with an abundance of caution and that things would go on as normal very shortly. Susan wished she felt as confident.

The door flew open and a policeman entered, leading a German Shepherd.

"We're almost done going through the school." He let the dog sniff the library. When it came near Duke, it growled, causing Duke to recoil.

"Don't you put muzzles on them things?" He rubbed his previous dog-inflicted injury.

The officer ignored him, allowing the dog to finish its search.

Janet said, "We're all safe. They'll be done any minute now."

"Looks like we're all clear in here." The police unit left, and the students immediately started texting.

"Cool," said Chad. "It's all over Instagram. There's the kid getting arrested and there's the policeman with the dog."

The principal's voice startled them as he announced the end of the 'Code Black' over the PA system.

"Thank God," said Janet. "You don't have to stay."

"And miss all the adventure? Not a chance." Susan grabbed a handful of red and green Hershey's kisses off Janet's desk, left a message for Mike now that her phone worked, and took a seat behind the circulation desk.

Chapter 13

When Susan walked through her front door, the aroma of garlic tickled her nose. "Audrey, are you making dinner?"

"It's on the table. Mike's in here helping me."

She hung up her coat and joined them in the kitchen. "What a first day back. The police came with the canine unit. Arrested two students and found a stash in the boy's locker room. Word is it was Fentanyl, the same thing Jordan and Richard were dealing."

"It was all over the news. I couldn't relax until I finally got your message. You had me worried sick." Mike gave her a warm hug.

Audrey said, "Richard's legacy lives on." She dished out the casserole. "You know, when you were both gone, a strange thing happened. I peeked outside the door to get the mail, and there was a dark sedan parked across the street. The driver was slumped down in the seat like he didn't want to be seen. As soon as I went inside, I heard the engine start and through the window saw it speeding away."

Susan grabbed a measuring cup so she could accurately track her food. "Did you copy down the plate number? What was the make and model?"

"Susan, it was across the street and I wasn't wearing my distance glasses. Do you think it has something to do with my trial?"

Mike took a second helping. "Maybe it was a reporter trying to catch you going out of the house. I wouldn't worry."

While they were eating, Lynette called to tell Susan the button she'd found was a dead end. No prints. *Was the driver parked across the street earlier the same person who'd lost the button in the driveway? What's so interesting about our house?*

"Susan, do you want to take an after dinner walk?" Mike had been pushing her to exercise ever since the diabetes diagnosis.

"It's freezing out."

"It'll make us walk faster. Besides, I heard about a study that found fewer cases of diabetes in people who lived in colder climates. Something about brown fat, white fat, purple fat. We'll have to ask Evan about it."

"I'll clean up the kitchen," said Audrey. "Wish I could go with you."

Susan changed into sweats over thermal underwear, then zipped up her ski jacket. "Let's go."

The neighbors were inside, eating dinner. She wondered why they left their curtains open like that. Anyone could see in. She could see her breath as she talked to Mike. "You don't think Audrey killed Richard, do you?"

"Do you? I can't imagine her pulling the trigger. Besides, she had all that time back in Florida to kill him. Why wait and do it where her family would have to see it."

"It's not making sense. The drug dealing is going on without Richard. I don't think there's motive there. And the police are surely keeping their eyes on Jordan Chadwick."

"What about Richard's cellmate? The dog groomer."

"Again, where's the motive?" She picked up the pace in an effort to warm up.

"What are the usual motives—money, revenge, love…"

"Love? Carmella and Bruce were sitting elbow to elbow at the bookstore that day. What if Bruce was jealous because Richard was carrying on with Carmella?"

They turned around at the end of the street and headed back home. Mike stopped in his tracks. "Look behind those trees. Do you see a car?"

She struggled to see. "Yes, I think you're right. Can you tell what color it is?" They creeped closer.

"Looks like a dark blue sedan to me." Mike squinted. "No, it's black. Someone's in the driver's seat. What's he doing? I'll bet it's a reporter, or a private investigator hired by the prosecutor. I'll call Lynette."

By the time he took off his glove and retrieved his phone from his pocket, the car drove away. "Kind of cool, huh? Like being stalked by the paparazzi."

"Hardly. Let's speed it up. I'm freezing."

They settled down in the living room with mugs of Swiss Miss. Mike turned on *Jeopardy*.

"I think we saw the same car you did," said Susan. "Mike is convinced it's a reporter or a private eye."

"I can't imagine who else it'd be. Could you do me a favor? My book is there in my tote bag. Would you hand it to me?"

Susan opened the bag. "I don't see it."

"Oh, maybe I left it on the dresser."

"I'll get it. It's a commercial. Besides, I need my warm socks." She went into the guestroom and immediately spotted the book. When she picked it up, a business card fell out. *Carmella's Boutique. When would Audrey have been there? Certainly not after we discovered Carmella was Snookems.*

Mike yelled up the stairs. "It's back on."

Audrey said she had no idea about Snookems until the night Richard was murdered. She surely didn't have the opportunity to go to the boutique after she was arrested. Maybe we've had this all wrong and the killer is right downstairs.

She stomped down the stairs. "Audrey."

"Did you get my book?"

"Yes, and look what I found inside. You told me you found out about *Snookems* the night of Richard's murder."

"That's right."

"Then why was her card tucked in your book?" She showed it to Audrey.

Audrey turned pale. "What do you mean? I have no idea how that card wound up in my book. Richard must have put it there before he died."

"Seriously? He was trying to tip you off that he was having an affair and even gave you the woman's address and phone number?"

Audrey shouted. "What are you accusing me of, Susan? Knowing my husband was unfaithful? Tracking down his mistress? What?"

Mike stood between them. "Now, ladies. I'm sure there's a perfectly logical explanation."

"I don't have one, but I can assure you I didn't put that card in there." Audrey folded her arms and plopped back onto the sofa.

Susan went into the kitchen and grabbed a handful of pretzel sticks from the pantry. The doorbell caused her to jump, dropping the entire handful onto the floor. She ran back into the living room.

"Are you expecting someone?" said Mike.

"No. Don't open it. It could be a robber or worse."

Mike peered through the peephole but the person was out of the line of view. He shouted, "Who's there?"

"Ask for ID," said Audrey.

This time, the visitor knocked. "If you don't tell me who it is, I'm not opening this door," said Mike.

"It's me."

"Me who? Is this some sort of a joke?" Mike again looked through the peephole. His face softened and he flung open the door.

Audrey's hands flew to her mouth. Susan simply shook her head. Johann leaped off the back of the couch where he'd been napping.

"Surprise!"

"George!" Audrey threw her arms around him. "What are you doing here? You said in your email you were on the way back to Florida."

"I am, or rather I was. I took off a few more days so I could check on you and see if you were okay."

"Come in. Have a seat. We had a heck of a time trying to contact you after Audrey was arrested."

"I was off the grid. No internet in the middle of the rainforest. Who knew."

Susan made coffee and offered George leftovers from dinner. She and Audrey filled him in.

"So, I find out Richard's having an affair because I see a text from a *Snookems*. He didn't even bother denying it. Then I take a taxi to the bed and breakfast down the road. After all, I couldn't stand to look at him. The next day, I go back to pack my things and when I go into the hotel room, there's Richard, dead on the floor. Then the police come and next thing I know I'm being arrested."

"Why do they think you did it? That good for nothing Richard had lots of enemies, I'm sure."

Susan cleared her throat. "I guess it's because of the smoking gun. Not literally smoking, but Audrey's prints were all over the gun."

"It was Richard's gun but we had it registered under my name. My prints were all over it because I'm the one who packed it."

"Do they have witnesses?"

Mike chimed in. "Yeah. The taxi driver who took Audrey to the bed and breakfast swears he returned her to the Holiday Inn later that night."

"But the mistress is a dead ringer for Audrey. The taxi driver himself says it could have been *Snookems* he drove the second time." Susan poured the coffee. "We also have a witness who saw Bruce Feinstein, Richard's old cellmate, going into the Holiday Inn after Audrey left."

George's phone vibrated. "Excuse me, I have to take this." George walked out onto the back porch.

What's so urgent. He's still on vacation after all.

"Susan, did you hear me? I said do you think George can help us?"

"I don't know. Let's hope so."

Chapter 14

"Did you sleep well?" asked Audrey. "I was so excited to see my son that it took me hours to settle down and fall asleep. I know he'll be able to help us."

Susan sprayed the frying pan with Pam and broke open an egg. "George hated Richard. He'll probably want to find and congratulate his killer." She filled the cats' water bowl while cooking. When she set it down, she noticed a leather wallet on the floor under the table. "Hey, I think George left his wallet behind. He won't get far without it. I'll drop it off on my way to school. He's at the Holiday Inn where you and Richard stayed, right?"

"Yes, that's what he said. George had been trying to get me to leave Richard ever since Richard was released from prison. I should have listened to him. Instead, look where I am now. Accused of murder. I feel like I'll wake up from this nightmare at any moment, but morning after morning I open my eyes and the whole mess is still in front of me. I can't go to prison. I'll kill myself first."

"Audrey! Stop your nonsense. You're not going to prison. I'll stop by Jonathan's and see if he's made any headway into the case."

Susan called Janet from the car to tell her she'd be a little late. When she stepped outside, she pulled her scarf tighter. The winter air bit like an angry dog. The gray sky with its low clouds made her want to crawl back into her bed. When she was working, she barely noticed the weather, but since retiring, her mood had become too easily influenced by temperature and cloud cover.

I should ask George what he knows about the drug situation in Westbrook. Working for the DEA, he has bigger fish to fry, but I can get his take on whether or not Richard was still involved after he was nailed for dealing. Let go on a technicality. Richard was a conman and a snake through and through. She pulled into the hotel parking lot. Curiosity always got the better of her. She was compelled to snoop through her half-brother's wallet before returning it, telling herself she'd get to see real Costa-Rican money left over from his trip.

No foreign currency. Did he exchange every last peso before arriving? Hmm, American Express Platinum, a couple of crisp twenties...a receipt from Avis. It's dated back before Christmas. On a hunch, she walked around the parking lot looking for cars with rental plates. There were few guests, being it was after the holidays. Folks seeking a mid-winter vacation were more likely to go skiing in Vermont than to hang out in the Hudson Valley when the trees were bare.

She passed a large SUV with an Avis sticker. *Nah.* She made her way through the next row. Bingo. A dark sedan with rental plates. *This looks just like the one I saw following me...and the one Mike and I saw on our street last night. If George just arrived, why has he had this rental for weeks, and why was he following me?*

She walked toward the hotel entrance, then stopped cold. *What's he doing here? That's him, I'm sure.* She took a step closer and adjusted her bifocals. *It's...Jordan Chadwick!* She ducked down behind a Ford Escape and watched Jordan pull away in his Jaguar. Shivering, she hustled toward the door.

A young woman worked the front desk. "Excuse me. I'm looking for my brother. He's a guest here. George Roberts."

"Oh, you're George's sister. He said he was visiting family. He's in Room 202. You can use the house phone to let him know you're here."

George opened the door dressed in a turtle neck and heavy jeans, his hair damp from the shower. A single suitcase lay open on the folding rack.

"Thanks for bringing this by. I hadn't realized I'd dropped it."

"I knew you'd need it." She pulled the bedspread taut and sank into the marsh-mallowy bed when she took a seat. "Audrey said you had back trouble. Sleeping on this won't help." She pulled out the desk chair. "How does Audrey seem to you?"

"Stressed, but in a way, she's ...well... more relaxed than when she was living with Richard. Back in Florida, she couldn't sleep, couldn't eat half the time."

"You don't think she..."

"Think she killed him? Nah. She'd have done it long ago if she was up to it. You'd have to be comfortable with using a gun, and Mom was anything but."

"George, have you heard anything about the drug ring resurfacing here in Westbrook?"

"No. I've been on vacation, and besides, the cases I get are on a larger, national scale. Not saying it isn't a problem. Opioids are big business everywhere."

She looked at her watch. "I'd better get going. I'm supposed to be volunteering at the school. Come by for dinner later?"

"Sure. Let me know what I can bring."

He's up to something. What business has he got with Jordan Chadwick? No, it couldn't be. She admonished herself for even thinking they were working together. *He was in town keeping an eye on Audrey and didn't want to seem like he was hovering. I'm sure that's all it was.*

She called Jonathan to see if he'd be home, then called Janet to say she'd be late. She remembered her doctor's appointment this afternoon, dreading hearing the verdict. Would she or would she not need to start medication to lower her blood sugar?

She pulled into La Puebla, noticing a backyard-swing set, a parka-clad man walking a sweater-clad terrier, and a child-sized plastic playhouse as she drove to Jonathan's. The neighborhood radiated warmth in spite of the temperature. She pulled into the driveway. *I'm so happy Jonathan decided to move here.*

Jonathan opened the front door "Hey, Susan." he gave her a peck on the cheek. "Come on in."

She hung her coat on the rack in the entranceway. "You put up the painting Lynette and Jason got you for Christmas. The colors liven up the room."

"It was Janet's idea to put it there over the table. Hey, look what I found." He picked up a legal pad from the table. "Bruce has a history dealing drugs dating back to his teenage days. He was going by a different name."

"Interesting, but not surprising."

"Here's something I wanted you to see." He handed her a printed copy of a newspaper article. "A well-known dealer was arrested and implicated both Bruce and Richard. He claims Bruce worked from Westbrook while Richard worked out of Banyan Beach. Thing is, the dealer testified he paid a grand sum to these guys, bank records verified he made a large withdrawal, backing up his story."

"Did they look at Richard and Bruce's financials?"

"No trace of the money, and no drugs found on either of them during a search."

"Bruce doesn't look as though he's rolling in it, with the dog salon and all. However, he's got a bunch of guard dogs at the groomers. I wonder what he's guarding." Some piece of information haunted her, but she couldn't remember what it was. *I know or heard something related to this.*

"Susan, you okay?"

"Yes. Wait a minute. I heard Richard talking to someone on the phone when they were at our house. I heard him say something like, 'Calm down. You know I don't have it.' He may have been talking to Bruce. I'll ask Lynette what she thinks."

Jonathan's phone vibrated. "It's the jewelry store."

She heard excitement in his voice. When he finished, he was grinning.

"The jewelry store owner located the receipt for the ring I found. His patient wife dug through the old filing cabinet and found it! We have a name!"

Chapter 15

The magnetic pull of the dog groomer lured her Prius away from Westbrook High. She was going to call Lynette, but she just wanted a quick look around the grounds to see if she could find evidence of drug dealing which would give Bruce a motive. Nothing dangerous. She called Janet to say she wouldn't be coming in and would see her tomorrow. When she arrived at Feinstein's, only one car was parked in the driveway. *I can't very well show up again without a dog.* She parked down the road and crept toward the backyard. She wasn't sure what she expected to find. As she got closer, one of the dogs barked like a maniac.

"Who's out there?" Susan heard Bruce's voice before he came into view. She dodged behind a tree, holding her breath. She wished she hadn't left her purse with her phone in the car.

"Come out or I'll let the dogs loose," said Bruce.

Susan felt the hair on the back of her neck tingle. If she made a run for it, could she escape? She heard the metal gate clang, then a crescendo of barking like a wave rolling into the shore. *It's now or never. One, two, three!* She ran for the car. Her heart pounded, and her legs gave way beneath her. *Oh, no.* The guard dog was inches in front of her. *What now?* She looked up into Bruce's face.

"Gottcha." He grabbed her by the sleeve and pulled her to her feet, leash wound tightly around his hand. His breath reeked of beer. "Let's go." He pushed her toward the house. The guard dog salivated and every time

Susan pulled back, Bruce snapped her forward. He dragged her through the dirty snow.

"Let me go! My daughter is a detective and she knows I'm here." Her pants were wet from the snow. He dragged her through the back door, into the house.

"Yeah, right." He duct-taped her hands together and tied her arms to a chair in the dog grooming area.

"Let me..." She felt the sticky tape on her lips as he sealed her mouth shut. She thought hard about how to escape, but hardly had enough play in the rope to even turn her taped wrists. *Why was I so stupid? I thought I'd conquered my impulsivity. Lynette and Mike will be furious. Think, Susan.*

Bruce's phone blared the theme from *Rocky*.

"Yeah. Tonight. Ten grand. Scarface. Got it."

I'll bet Scarface is code for Fentanyl. She scanned the room. One measly sink with a bottle of dog shampoo next to it. A few dirty towels. Empty wire cages. On the wall, chain leashes and large, riveted collars that she couldn't imagine fitting a prissy Maltese or Poodle. Then she spotted it. A pair of wire cutters near the cages. *If I can wriggle over to them and somehow get them into my hands...*

The bell over the front door signaled a visitor. She tried to scream but her jaws may as well have been wired shut.

"Don't go anywhere. I'll be right back." He laughed as he exited though the curtain into the reception area.

Think, Susan. Focus. She bounced on the chair, moving it by inches nearer to the wire cutters. She tried to speed it up, but she needed time. *Almost there.* She prayed he couldn't hear the chair thumping against the tile. She could hear Bruce talking. A nasally baritone voice answered him.

"I want five big ones on Scarface for tonight. He better come through for me."

"You got nothing to worry about."

"Yeah, you're right. I cleaned up last time. Been spreading the word, too."

"Appreciate the business referral."

The man with the baritone voice said, "And here. This is from Ace. Same. Put it on Scarface. We're still on for tonight, right?"

"Yeah. Park around back."

Worried he'd be back any second, Susan evaluated her current plan and realized she'd never make it to the counter in time. Then she remembered a trick she'd seen about breaking free of duct tape. Only it involved holding her arms above her head and slicing down. Tied to the chair, it was impossible. Footsteps trudging closer. She wished she hadn't canceled her volunteering. If only she'd let it go at being late, Janet would have sent the troops looking for her by now. The door creaked open.

"So you think you're clever. Guess you'll be needing more like maximum security. Now, what should I do with you?" said Bruce.

Susan mumbled through her taped mouth and frantically bobbed her head toward the exit.

"Oh, yeah. I've the perfect place for you." He released her hands and re-taped them behind her back. "On your feet."

She tried to resist standing, but he yanked her with such force, her bifocals fell to the ground. He pushed her from behind. *Is that a gun he has pressed against my back?* Her nerves felt like flames. Soon they were outside. Freezing cold. Without her glasses, she couldn't be sure, but it looked like he was pushing her toward a wire fenced area. Dogs barked as he pushed her closer. Now she could see it was a long enclosure with a chain across the top. No…more like a pulley running across.

"The dogs got to get their exercise. Every hour I give them a little more leeway." He took her to the end of the enclosure and pulled a meat hook down from the pulley. "Now look at that. It fits right through that jacket you're wearing." He pierced the collar of her jacket, then taped her ankles together. "By this evening, Iron Jaw will make it close enough to have a hearty dinner."

Susan's head ached. Her legs felt like Slinkys. She imagined being let through the doors of the ancient colosseum with a hungry tiger waiting inside. *How am I ever going to get out of this one?*

Bruce hooked up Iron Jaw to the other end of the pulley, adjusted the resistance, and ripped the muzzle from his mouth. "There, boy. Work yourself up a good appetite. Lots of meat on that one." He laughed as he slammed the back door shut behind him.

"God, please get me out of this. My family needs me. I promise I'll be nicer to Audrey." She was sweating despite the temperature. Her wet pant legs from when Bruce dragged her into the house stuck to her skin. Now, to make things worse, it was snowing and she couldn't wipe the melted flakes off her face. She heard a pickup truck pull into the driveway, but whoever it was wouldn't see her. A short time later, she heard it drive away.

He's got some business going. Three deals in the amount of time she'd been here. The ugly Pit Bull growled and ran right up as far as he was able. He was still about ten feet away. She wondered how fast he'd make it to her end of the enclosure.

She pictured Annalise and Mia. Just the other day she'd taken them to the mall and they'd run into Stephanie's mother with her therapy dog. Mia started crying, and Annalise hid behind her leg. She'd told Annalise not to be scared—that dogs are friendly. *He won't hurt you.* She knew you shouldn't pet a therapy dog, but Stephanie's mother said it was fine and she held Annalise's hand so they could pet her together. When they got home, the first words out of her mouth to Lynette were, 'Please, can we get a dog?' Never again would she view dogs the same way.

Another engine. Sounded like a motorcycle. *Please, God, let him come out here and find me.* No luck. Again, the *customer* spent a few minutes inside, then she heard him take off. Her head felt light and she knew her blood sugar was dropping. Then things turned black and a warmth overcame her.

When she awoke, the dog had made significant progress toward her, and the gray outline of the sun dropped behind the mountain. Her head throbbed and she couldn't think clearly. *Please, God. Let me find a way out of here.*

Did she imagine it, or did she hear footsteps outside the enclosure? *Mike! How did he find her?*

Like a knight riding in on a white horse, he squeezed through an opening in the enclosure and ran to her. "Susan! Thank God I found you. Stay still. Let me get you out of here."

He pulled the tape off her feet, then started working on freeing her hands. "I've almost got it."

Susan's heart raced. She tried to scream, forgetting her mouth was still taped. Her eyes opened wide and she held her breath as she watched Mike slump into a heap at her feet.

Chapter 16

Lynette burst through the front door of her mother's house, fists tensed, as if to contain her anger. "Audrey, did she say where she was going? What about Dad?"

"Don't yell at me. I don't know, that's why I called you. She went to school this morning. At least, I think she did."

"But she didn't come home. And what about my Dad?"

"She wasn't here when he got home. He got a call saying Susan missed her doctor's appointment. Then he called Janet, I think. And Jonathan. Then he grabbed his keys and ran out. Do you think she's all right?"

"When she didn't come home at the normal time, didn't you wonder where she was?"

"I figured she stopped at the store or something. You know, she invents excuses not to be around me. Then I got a call from her doctor's office saying she never showed up. That's when I called you."

Lynette tried her mother, but it went straight to voicemail. Same thing when she tried her dad.

"See, she doesn't answer."

"Let me call Jonathan." Her fingers punched the numbers. He picked up after the first ring.

"What's wrong? Yes, she stopped by this morning. I thought she was going to school. Yes, we talked about the case. I told her about the drug dealer who implicated Bruce and Richard, and she thought it was strange Bruce owned the groomers if he had a stash of drug money. Then I got a call from the guy at the jewelry store. Guess I wasn't concentrating when she left. Do you think she's okay? Did she make it to Westbrook High? She didn't get into an accident, did she? The roads are a little slick."

"I checked. No accidents. Now my Dad's missing. I'm going to try Janet."

"Please keep me in the loop. I'm worried now."

Lynette relayed the parts of the conversation Audrey didn't hear, then called Janet.

"No, Lynette. She called and said she'd be late, then later called and said she wasn't coming at all."

Lynette grabbed her coat. "I'm going to call Jackson. I have an idea where she might be."

It was dark by the time Mike regained consciousness. Susan felt his body hanging limply behind her. On high alert, her ears searched for the sound of him breathing. The dog was now only a foot or two away. His pointy teeth stood out against the dark. Every time he growled, Susan felt her heart stop, sure she was about to be ripped to pieces. She'd seen Bruce coming with the shovel in his hand, creeping up on Mike. Then, whack. The sound of him hitting Mike's head stung through her like a poison arrow. She waited.

Mike kicked her with his bound legs and she thanked God he was conscious. Her whole body shook and her head throbbed. At least if she was going to die, she'd die with Mike. *What the heck am I thinking. I can't die. Neither can Mike. Not tonight.* She looked at Iron Jaw staring her in the face, salivating. There had to be a way…

"Turn here," said Lynette. "I called Evan and he said the groomer was off this road."

Jackson turned on the siren and skidded on the icy dirt road. "There. Come on. What's with all the pickup trucks and motorcycles? Call for backup."

Lynette jumped out of the car before Jackson could turn off the engine. She ran to the door and turned the knob, then yelled back to Jackson, "It's unlocked. Come on." They searched the kitchen, the hall closet, the living room...

"Let's check upstairs. They have to be somewhere." Jackson led the way. They checked the closets, under the beds, behind the shower curtain...

"Nothing. All those cars and no sign of life?"

"They're somewhere on the grounds," said Jackson.

"Wait. The basement!" They flew back down the staircase to the basement door. Lynette pulled her keychain flashlight out of her pocket. "Look, a dirty handprint. It's still wet." They descended the creaky steps. Lynette aimed the beam of light strategically over the walls and floor. "No one's here."

"Wait," said Jackson. "Over there. There's light coming from under that door."

"I hear something."

They readied their weapons and listened at the door.

"What's all the yelling and screaming?"

"We're about to find out." Lynette charged through the door. "Hands up."

Makeshift bleachers surrounded a dirt rink. Two bloody Pit Bulls ripped at each other while the small crowd roared. Back-up had arrived quickly. Several officers charged into the room and rounded up the spectators. Lynette grabbed Bruce. "Pull your dogs off each other. Now!"

Bruce and the officers separated the animals.

"So that's what this place is all about. Dog fighting!" Jackson locked the dogs in separate cages after Bruce slapped muzzles on them.

"If that no good ex-partner of mine had given me my share of the drug loot, I wouldn't a had to resort to this. He owes me! Who wound up with it anyway? That wife of his? I know he stiffed Jordan Chadwick too, but that kid's rolling in his parent's inheritance. Me, I gotta make a living, and giving spa treatment to dogs wasn't gonna cut it."

"If you tell us where the drugs are hidden, maybe they'll go easy on you. Is that why you killed Richard Stirling, your former cell mate and partner in crime?"

"Killed him? Not me. He was alive when I went over to his hotel and begged for my share of the loot. I wasn't gonna get my hands on it if he was dead, now was I? I'll tell you who I did see. That prissy wife of his. She was angry too. Didn't even notice me when she passed me in the lobby. She's the one you should be accusing."

"Where's my mother?"

"You mean that snoopy broad with the whiny voice. Good luck."

"Get him outta here," said Lynette.

They went back upstairs. "Mom, are you here?" She ran into the kitchen, then into the grooming salon. "Look! These are her glasses on the floor. She's here somewhere."

"Let's check outside," said Jackson.

"Do you hear that? It's another dog!"

They ran outside and followed the barking. Lynette led the way.

"Over there." Then she screamed," Mom! Dad!"

Iron Jaw was less than a foot away from her parents. "Jackson, stop that dog!"

Susan's knees stopped trembling when she saw Lynette. She'd been sure this was the end and she'd never see her family again.

While Jackson yanked the pulley, dragging the dog back to the other end of the enclosure, Lynette ran to her parents. "Are you okay?" She ripped the duct tape off Susan's mouth. "Jackson, help me get them down." Susan's mouth stung like a sunburned albino.

Jackson pressed his glove against the bleeding wound on Mike's head. Working together, he and Lynette freed them both. "Mike, can you hear me? Are you okay?"

"I think so." He reached for his head, but Jackson pushed his hand away, still pressing his glove against the wound. "Susan?"

Her cheeks were numb from the cold. "I'm right here. Thank God you found us. Another few minutes and Iron Jaw would'a had the meal of his life. Did you find the drugs?"

"No, Mom. We searched the place. No drugs. We discovered a dog fighting ring. That's how Bruce was making his money."

"Dog fighting? No drugs?"

"Sounds like he was out of the drug partnership after Richard and Jordan got caught. Richard owed him money, though."

"There's his motive."

"No, he needed Richard alive if he was ever to get his share. He says he saw Audrey at the hotel that night."

"It was Carmella. The taxi driver said he couldn't be sure if he'd driven Audrey or Carmella back to the hotel. They look an awful lot alike."

"And why was Carmella visiting Richard?"

"She was *Snookem*s. Remember? They were having an affair."

Chapter 17

Susan spent most of the next day relaxing on the sofa with Ludwig and Johann. She was surprised to learn that Duke, the substitute shop teacher from the media center, was one of the people arrested for participating in the dog fights. *So that's how he got the dog bite he had bandaged.*

Lynette verified that when Bruce left Richard's hotel, Richard was still alive. She checked room service receipts. Richard had ordered a bottle of wine *after* the close circuit footage showed Bruce leaving the hotel, but *before* Carmella came in. Mike slept in and went to work for a few hours in the afternoon. Starting to feel restless after watching too many talk shows, Susan plodded upstairs and exchanged her sweats for yoga pants and a long sleeved t-shirt.

"Audrey, I'm going over to Jonathan's. I'll be back before dinner."

"Are you sure you're up to it? I can't imagine how horrible it was going through what you did."

"I need to get my mind off it. Besides, I told Janet I'd be in all day tomorrow to help her in the media center, and won't have a chance to check on the case. Why don't you call George and invite him over for dinner?"

"I will. I was hoping he'd come by this afternoon anyway."

Susan hopped in her blue Prius. *Bruce didn't kill Richard. He and Jordan Chadwick were dealing drugs as a team before Jordan and Richard were caught.*

Bruce said Richard owed them money. That brings it full circle with Jordan Chadwick once again a suspect.

When Susan pulled into Jonathan's driveway, he was shoveling yesterday's snow off the front stoop. She was proud that her 80-year-old father had the stamina and desire to shovel snow. Dressed in a plaid jacket topped off with the red scarf and hat Janet had given him for his birthday, he looked twenty years younger. *Hope I inherited his genes!* He smiled as she came nearer.

"Susan, let's go in. My hands are getting numb." He leaned the shovel against the side of the house and stomped the snow off his boots. Susan scraped her shoes on the cheerful welcome mat, then followed Jonathan into the house. The sterile new house had become a cozy home. Colorful throw pillows brightened the beige sofa, and African violets on the window ledge peeked out behind checkered café curtains, basking in the sun coming through the kitchen window. "Do I smell potpourri?"

"Janet's idea. It's from Yankee Candle. Plugs into the outlet." He pointed toward the outlet on the floor. The kitchen table was littered with legal pads full of notes.

Susan cleared a space and had a seat. She tried to read the notes, but Jonathan's handwriting was nearly illegible.

"You've been a busy bee."

"I've been working on Audrey's case most of the day. Bruce has been ruled out as a suspect. Jordan Chadwick is iffy. Don't think he could be running a drug business by himself while also running Agrowmex."

"What if he had help? What if he had another partner we don't know about?"

"Are you saying yet another partner is in cahoots with Jordan Chadwick?"

"Well, when you say it out loud it sounds rather remote. I'm grasping at straws."

"I'm concentrating on the Carmella angle. We have to prove she was at the hotel the night of the murder and it wasn't Audrey the cab driver drove there later that night. She has a flimsy alibi. Her family says they went to church and had dinner together, but no one at the church remembers seeing her at midnight mass."

Changing the subject, she said, "So tell me what you found out about the ring. You sounded excited on the phone."

Jonathan poured two mugs of coffee. "I talked to the jewelry store owners. They found a receipt."

"That's great news!"

"Pop, the designer, will be there this afternoon. Ma said to come by and talk to him."

"Well, what are we waiting for?"

They jumped into Susan's Prius. The neighborhood was quiet this time of day. After yesterday's snow, the sun was trying to break through, and snow drifts along the sides of the road were beginning to melt.

"Are you okay after yesterday?" asked Jonathan.

"Glad it's over. If I preferred cats over dogs before, yesterday cinched it. We're going to the jewelry store downtown, right?"

"Yep. You know, I was relying on Bruce Feinstein for reasonable doubt."

"I still say Jordan is a viable option."

"He would be, if he was hurting for money. He's well dressed, the CEO of a company...it'll be a hard sell to the jury."

"Audrey said Jordan came to the hotel to speak to Richard the day before the murder. She just remembered that."

"So? We can't place him there the night of the murder. Hey, isn't that the turn for the jewelry store?"

Susan found a parking place between the store and Barnes and Noble. Remembering how difficult it was to park the last time she was downtown after a snowstorm, she was relieved the plows had been by earlier. When they entered the store, the owner was finishing up with a customer.

"This shop was one of the original downtown stores," said Susan. "It's been in their family since it was built." Shiny engagement rings on velvet backing sparkled under the glass. A display case on the wall sported estate jewelry. The owner rung up a rose gold watch for a customer, who thanked him profusely for steering him to the perfect birthday present for his wife. The bell over the door tinkled as he left. The gray-haired man with wire glasses turned his attention to them.

"Jonathan Stirling, right? We spoke on the phone. And you I already know." The elderly owner smiled at Susan and said to Jonathan, "This one's been a customer as long as I can remember."

"The best jewelry store in town," said Susan. "Jonathan says you have a lead on the ring he found."

Jonathan handed Pop the ring.

"Oh, yes. That's my work all right."

"It's beautiful. I hate to think how awful the owner must have felt losing it. Thanks for getting back to me. What do you remember about this ring?"

"That ring had a sweet story behind it. The buyer was a young guy, Dylan McHenry. It was during the draft era and he was afraid his number would be coming up. Came to me asking if I could design an artsy-looking engagement ring for his 'soulmate.' They were both young, but he didn't want to go off to Vietnam without letting her know his intentions."

"Did he say who this soulmate was?"

"No, just the initial I engraved in it. Her name or pet name started with a *D*. He picked it up late one afternoon. Said he was going to propose that night."

"Did he ever get back with you, to have it sized or cleaned?" Susan was hopeful.

"No, but strange thing. A few days later, I heard he was missing. I'd been one of the last people to see him. Police came by asking questions."

"Did they find him?" asked Jonathan.

"Or his body?" asked Susan. The two men gave her a quizzical look.

"They never found him. Or his body. Speculation was he ran off to Canada to avoid the war. I guess his soulmate never did know his intentions."

"Do you happen to have an address for him? I know it's been a long time." Jonathan loosened his scarf. The colder it was outside, the stuffier it seemed to be indoors.

The designer pulled a receipt out of his pocket. "Don't know if it'll be of any help, but here you go."

Jonathan took the receipt, then glanced at the rings under the glass.

Feeling a twinge of excitement, Susan said, "Are you thinking of buying one for Janet? That one is gorgeous." She smudged the glass pointing it out.

Jonathan's face turned redder than the scarf he was wearing. "Um, not right now. We haven't been going out long." Susan thought his eyes sparkled for a moment as she followed him out of the shop.

She couldn't resist the bookstore, and her stomach was growling for a late afternoon snack. After all, it was right across the street. "How about I treat you to a cup of coffee?"

Jonathan responded quickly, "Sounds good to me."

A display of bright, hard-covered, *expensive as far as she was concerned,* best sellers greeted them at the entrance. Susan browsed through the new releases, pausing to read the back of a romance novel, then headed to the mystery section. Jonathan grabbed a new spy thriller. They bought coffee and shared an oversized chocolate chip muffin in the café.

"After this, let's drive by the address we got. Wouldn't it be amazing to return the ring to its owner. I wonder if the two of them ever got together."

"How cool if he could give her the ring all these years later." She chipped away at her half of the muffin. Eating little bites and sharing off one plate made her feel less guilty about the carb count. *That reminds me. I have to make a new doctor's appointment.*

Jonathan pulled his iPhone from his pocket. "Let's see who lives at that address now. Susan, are you okay?"

"Hey, that's Jordan Chadwick." She instinctively softened her voice.

"Where?"

"On the bench by the magazines. This isn't the first time I've seen him here." She sipped her coffee, then almost spit it back out. "George! What's my brother doing here? Look. He sat down next to Jordan Chadwick."

"It could be a coincidence."

"No. Look. They're talking to each other. What's he putting into his phone?"

"Let's go over and find out."

"No." Her suspicions grew as she remembered how George happened to have winter clothes in his suitcase after a trip to the rainforest. *Is George involved in the drug dealing? With Jordan?* She further began to wonder why he hadn't contacted Audrey over the holidays. Surely there was internet service somewhere in the rainforest. If he was even there at all.

"Susan, I have a fairly suspicious mind, but yours is on overdrive. Just because they're sitting together, talking, doesn't mean they have a relationship."

Feeling guilty for immediately suspecting her brother, she said, "I'll bet George is keeping tabs on Jordan. That's why he was here."

Susan slumped down in her seat while she watched George walk out the front entrance. A few minutes later, Jordan left. She pressed her fork down against the plate and licked up every last crumb.

Jonathan turned his attention back to his phone. "Voila. The residence lists a Colonel William and Barbara McHenry. Must be Dylan's parents."

"I'm surprised they're still alive."

"Hey! If Dylan is more or less your age, his parents may be more or less mine. Let's go."

Chapter 18

"Susan, I doubt they're going to answer the door to strangers. What are we going to say to them?"

"We'll tell them you found the ring and we traced it back to their son, Dylan. For all we know, he himself lives there now."

"Or the place was sold years ago."

"No, we googled it, remember? Right after we got his name at the shop."

"It would be quite something if we found him. There, the street is on the left."

The McHenrys lived in one of the oldest sections of town, near the railroad bridge. Their house was brick with white trim, flanked by large, bare Maple trees with ice-coated branches. A wooden mailbox on a painted stand marked the end of the driveway.

"Careful, don't slip," said Jonathan. They took a step up to the front door. "I wonder why they added that ramp?"

Susan rang the doorbell and they waited.

"Coming," they heard through the door. A white-haired lady in a housecoat answered the door. She had the bluest eyes Susan remembered ever seeing. "Can I help you?"

"I hope so. I'm Susan Wiles and this is my father, Jonathan Stirling."

"Oh, yes. The man at the jewelry store called and asked if it was okay to give out our address. Called back today and said to expect a visit. Come in."

They followed her into the living room and sat on a nubby plaid couch. Susan picked up an unusual glass ashtray from the coffee table.

"This is beautiful! Is this hand blown?"

"Yes, my son made it when he was in high school. He was very talented, even started selling some of his works at craft shows."

She picked up a photo of a teenager wearing a track uniform. "Is this your son?"

"Yes, that's Dylan." Mrs. McHenry shook the man snoozing in the recliner. "Wake up, Colonel. We have visitors."

Colonel. McHenry snapped awake, returning the recliner to its sitting position. "Yes, we heard you found some sort of ring?"

Jonathan took the ring from his pocket. "I found this outside behind my new house. Susan here says there used to be a private park in the same spot years ago. We think the ring belonged to your son, Dylan."

The woman took the ring. "Oh, my goodness. He must have bought this for Dee. We knew it was only a matter of time before he proposed. Then he got that draft notice."

"So he went to Vietnam?" said Jonathan.

The father continued. "He never went to no Vietnam. Dylan was a coward. He didn't want to fight for his country. The night before he was supposed to report he disappeared into thin air. Never heard from him again."

"My husband left him no choice. William was career military. Fought in both world wars. No son of his was going to dodge the draft, right, dear?"

"I didn't raise a coward. Bet he's living in Canada somewhere."

"He knows how angry William would be, even now. I just hope God has been good to him. I may very well have grandchildren I never got to meet." She turned to her husband. "I'll never forgive you for that."

Jonathan looked at Susan as if to say *maybe we shouldn't be here.* Susan broke the awkwardness.

"Dee. Do you know if she's still living in town? What's her last name?"

"I have no idea. We'd barely gotten to know her when the whole argument about fleeing the draft surfaced. She hated William for imposing his views on Dylan. The girl was a bit of a hippy. For all I know she's with him now. I prayed for all these years that was the case and poor Dylan hasn't been alone all this time."

William stood up. "See what you've gone and done? Opened old wounds. Take the ring. We don't want it. Dylan is dead to us."

Susan's heart broke, watching tears stream down Mrs. McHenry's cheeks. "I'm so sorry we've upset you. You won't be bothered by us again," said Susan. She wanted to take Dylan's mother aside and convince her to search for her son, but she knew it wasn't any of her business. Besides, how could she get Mrs. McHenry alone without her husband?

"Thanks for speaking with us. Sorry to have brought up a painful subject. I was just trying to return the ring to its owner, especially since it had sentimental value. Take care of yourselves." Jonathan pulled the door closed behind them. They were silent until they got back into the car.

"Jonathan, Dylan can't be too hard to find. Likely he's living in Canada."

"Canada's a big country. Besides, you saw how it upset his parents. We'll have to let sleeping dogs lie."

"I guess you have a point. But maybe Dee is…"

"Susan, let's not even go there. We have a case to focus on. That'll keep us plenty busy."

She turned on the car radio to distract herself from arguing with Jonathan about continuing the search for Dylan McHenry. Her thoughts drifted back to her brother.

"Jonathan, I found out that George was in town weeks before he says he arrived. I found a car rental receipt in with his things. He's been here since before Christmas. Since before Richard was murdered."

"Are you sure about that?"

"Yes. When I went to his hotel room, he had a huge suitcase filled with winter clothes. You don't take winter clothes to the rain forest now, do you?"

"No, but why would he have kept it a secret?"

"I don't know, but I think it was him who followed me in the black sedan, and who was outside our house New Year's Eve. The rental car was a black sedan. I saw it in the hotel parking lot."

They turned into Jonathan's neighborhood. Jonathan sat quietly for a while, then had an idea.

"Audrey said George hated Richard and was trying to convince her to leave him. He must have been worried sick about her, but knew Richard wouldn't put up with him following Audrey around. That's why he kept it a secret."

"I'm wondering what was really happening down in Banyan Beach. I'm thinking it may be worth a trip in the near future. Are you game?"

"I'm in."

Chapter 19

When Susan arrived home, Audrey was busy puttering in the kitchen. She'd forgotten to stop at ShopRite and remembered she'd invited George for dinner. *Time to forage through the closets and freezer.* Audrey looked especially relaxed and had even put on makeup.

"Audrey, what are you up to?"

"I'm so happy that George is here in New York. I'm planning dinner. I found chopped meat in the fridge and kidney beans in the closet. Thought I'd whip up some chili."

Susan said, "Great. I had no idea what to make. Hey, I think there's a box of Jiffy cornbread mix in the pantry." She waded through the shelves. "Here it is."

While Audrey sizzled the ground beef with chopped onions, Susan started the cornbread.

"Audrey, were George and Richard at least civil to each other?"

"George didn't make much of an effort to get to know Richard. He refused to come to our wedding, you know. Granted, we ran down to City Hall, but I had to drag my friend Pam with us so we'd have a witness. Mostly, they avoided each other."

"Do you think George could have killed Richard to protect you?"

"George? A killer? No way. He tried to persuade me to leave Richard, but murder him?"

She restrained herself from pushing the matter and turned her attention to the food. "Why are you adding green peppers? You don't put green peppers in chili."

"Of course you do. Gives them a bit of heat."

"Green peppers aren't hot."

"Yes they are. Who taught you how to cook anyway?"

Now she was fuming and could no longer contain herself. "My mother! That's who taught me, my real mother!" She heard the front door open.

"Susan, Audrey, something smells good." Mike plopped his lunch box down on the counter and gave Susan a kiss. "What's wrong?"

"Just a disagreement. Have you ever heard of putting green peppers in chili?"

Mike looked from his wife to Audrey. "I'm playing Switzerland on this one. With, without…" He picked up the wooden spoon and took a taste. "This is fantastic!" When he saw his wife's face, he added, "Um, the cornbread smells really good too. Susan always makes a great cornbread."

"It's from a mix," said Audrey.

Before Susan could throw the box at her, Audrey excused herself to go change, leaving the chili on the stove to simmer.

"Honey, I signed us up for something I think will be very beneficial. Not that I condone you getting in the middle of dangerous situations, but since you always seem to wind up there, I thought you should—we should—have some training."

"Training?"

"This guy came by the office today trying to get a permit for a gym. He's teaching out of his house but the business is growing."

"What kind of business?"

"He teaches self-defense. Not fancy martial arts or anything, just ways to get out of sticky situations. He showed me a few moves." Mike punched the air with the heel of his hand. "That's called a palm strike."

"Moves to escape a robber or a kidnapper or something?"

"Yeah. Even how to break free if someone has a weapon."

"Interesting. I'm in." *Maybe I can get a few Fit Bit points for doing it.*

Mike changed his clothes while Susan set the table and took the cornbread out of the oven. She snuck a taste of the chili. *Not bad but I'll never admit it.* She heard Audrey coming down the stairs just as the doorbell rang.

"I'll get it, Susan." Audrey gave George a big hug and brought him into the kitchen. He carried a white bakery box tied with string. "I bought an authentic New York cheesecake for dessert."

"How thoughtful. Isn't he thoughtful, Susan?"

"Yes, Audrey. Very thoughtful. Thank you, George." *Cheesecake has something like twenty Weight Watcher points and will most certainly spike my blood sugar.* She contemplated forgoing dessert, but if she did that, Mike would think she was mad with fever. She never turned down dessert.

George took an exaggerated sniff. "Something smells delicious. Did you make chili, Mom? I hope you put lots of peppers."

Mike, now dressed in well-worn jeans and a flannel shirt, took a liter of soda and a pitcher of cold water out of the fridge. "I'll set these on the table. George, Audrey, have a seat."

Susan had lots of questions for George and was cautious not to sound suspicious. She waited until the chili had been served and the drinks were poured.

"So, George, tell us more about the rainforest," said Susan. "Must be hot as blazes down there."

"Hot and humid. Felt like I was living in a shower."

"What made you decide to vacation there? I mean, this time of year I'd have thought you'd want to spend the holidays with your mother."

"To be truthful, I didn't want to spend them with Richard and I knew he and Mom were a package deal. Besides, I needed to unplug—take in some natural beauty." He took seconds of the chili before finishing what was on his plate.

Audrey said, "Speaking of natural beauty, have you been seeing anyone?"

Saved by the bell. George's phone vibrated. "Sorry, I have to take this." He went into the living room.

Susan was about to tell Audrey to mind her own business, but she would have done the same to Evan had he not been dating anyone. She scooped more chili onto her plate. *If he's on vacation and doesn't have a girlfriend, and his family is here in front of him, who's he talking to?*

She stood up from the table. "I'm getting more butter. Anyone want anything from the kitchen?"

Both Mike and Audrey shook their heads no. Susan went to the kitchen, took out the butter, and worked her way over to the wall that opened into the living room. She strained to hear George's end of the conversation.

"You told him? Tomorrow in front of the bookstore, right? We'll be cashing in on your good work real soon." George went back to the dining room.

Who's he talking to? Jordan Chadwick?

"Susan, where are you?"

"Coming, Mike. I'm going to start the coffee."

When she returned to the table, Mike was talking to George about the drug problem. "Susan was volunteering the other day and they arrested some kids right at the school. She was locked in the media center for hours. The police even brought in a canine unit."

"It's a problem all over. In Florida, the governor declared the opiate epidemic a state of emergency. We got federal funding but it's not enough. We keep putting out fires—arrest a small-time seller or kids buying the stuff. Unless we get the big guns it's not going to stop. And there's lots of layers between the little guy and the big time supplier."

"I'll bet those higher up the food chain are getting rich," said Susan.

"You can't even imagine. Enough talk about work. Is it time for dessert?"

What if George, Richard, and Jordan were running the show? That was eliminating Bruce, though he said Richard owed him money.

Audrey brought the cake to the table; Mike served the coffee. Johann had a sixth sense whenever creamy foods were being served and meowed at Susan's feet.

"So what's Jonathan say about Mom's case?"

"He's trying to pin reasonable doubt on another suspect. We've eliminated Bruce Feinstein, Richard's ex-cellmate. Close-circuit TV shows Richard was alive when he left on Christmas Eve. Jordan Chadwick visited Richard the day before he was murdered, but there's no proof he was there the night of the murder. You know Jordan, don't you, George?"

"Jordan Chadwick. Name sounds familiar, but I never met him." He cut himself a second piece of cheesecake.

"There's the mistress motive," said Mike. "*Snookems* may have gotten fed up with Richard's antics."

"And if he treated her the way he treated Audrey, well, let's say not many women would put up with it." Susan shot Audrey a disapproving look.

"Can't Jonathan pin it on her?" said George.

"Carmella has an alibi. She claims to have been at midnight mass with her daughter and son-in-law, but the taxi driver thinks he drove her to the hotel at around the time of the murder." Audrey slipped Johann a bite of cake under the table. "First he said it was me he drove, but Susan realized how similar we look and then the driver wasn't so sure."

"So, we 're left with two flimsy suspects, Jordan and *Snookems,*" said Susan. *And you, dear brother. You just denied knowing Jordan when I saw you talking to him at the bookstore. And you lied about being in the rainforest. You have two good motives. First, you could be profiting from the drug trade, and second, you wanted your mother to be safe from her abuser.*

"Between Jonathan and the police, I'm sure the truth will come out. It always does," said Mike.

"I agree," said Susan. "The truth will come out."

Chapter 20

Susan pulled on yoga pants and a long-sleeved shirt, hoping the attire was appropriate for the self-defense class. She was tickled that Mike cared enough to havesigned them up, and that he was beginning to accept her need to get in on the action when it involved defending her loved ones or the security of their hometown.

Mike called from the bottom of the steps. "Susan, you ready? I don't want to be late."

"Just grabbing my sneakers." She stifled a giggle when she went downstairs and saw Mike wearing a stretchy set of wrist bands and a matching headband. "Haven't you had those since the sixties?"

"They're still wearable. I don't want to get sweat in my eyes. Come on."

The class was held at Westbrook High's gymnasium. A few cars were parked out front.

"Tim, the instructor, says he made a deal with the school. He's teaching self-defense to the PE students in exchange for using the gym. He hopes to have his own place by next year," said Mike.

When they went inside, half a dozen others were sitting on the bleachers, waiting to start.

Tim was tall and broad-shouldered, slightly younger than Susan and Mike. His ebony biceps were the size of Susan's calves. He smiled a perfect smile. *That's a good sign. Someone in this field who still has his teeth—gives him credibility.*

Susan recognized all of the participants. Some were former students, one was someone she knew from the hair salon, and Della Hops, dressed in a tie-dyed shirt and vintage jeans.

"Hi, Della," said Susan. "Those tomatoes I bought from you last week were out of this world. Can't believe you manage to grow them in the middle of winter."

"It's all about the soil and keeping a proper temperature in the greenhouse."

"I hope I learn a few tricks. Mike wants me to keep safe when I but into situations I shouldn't," said Susan. "What brings you here?"

"Last week at the indoor flea market I was closing up and this thug follows me into the parking lot and grabs my knapsack. Got my wallet and my cash box. I'm not letting that happen again."

"Did the police catch him?"

"Naw. Said there'd been a string of purse snatchings. Cop said they've seen more robberies since the drug epidemic has grown. Let 'em try that again." She punched the air. A man about her age with an overgrown beard put his hand around Della's shoulders. "This is my friend, Neil."

"Nice to meet you," said Susan. "Is he your significant other?" Mike elbowed her.

"Neil? Naw, just a good friend. Only ever had one significant other in my life, the biggest disappointment ever. If there's anything I'm sure of, it's you gotta be able to take care of yourself—no one else will."

Tim stood in front of the class. "Everybody up. We're going to start with some stretches. Roll your shoulders forward, then back. That's it. This is a self-defense class. Self-defense isn't martial arts like you see on TV, and it's not a boxing match with a referee to make sure everyone's fighting fair. Self-defense means stopping the threat. You've gotta go from zero to a hundred and don't stop till the threat is gone."

Tim demonstrated a palm strike. "Now you try."

The class punched at the air, then Tim came around with a protective pad. "Give me a punch. Good power, Susan. That's it. Your turn, Mike. Remember, action is faster than reaction."

After learning several ways to disarm a potential attacker, the class stopped for a water break. Della was relaying her mugging story to a few participants, one of whom, Jack, was a friend Lynette had gone through the police academy with. After graduating, he had decided to go to law school and now worked for the district attorney.

Della said, "He snuck up behind me and, whammo, pulled my knapsack right off my shoulder. That ain't gonna happen again. I tell you, they need to clean up the drug problem in this town. It's at the root of all evil. Heck, I grew up in the sixties here. Back then, people didn't steal, they shared."

"I can't believe Jordan Chadwick weaseled his way out of a prison sentence. Out on a technicality, my foot," said Susan. "All our problems started when Agrowmex and the Chadwick family came to town."

Lynette's friend said, "There was no technicality. That arrest was right by the book. We had an airtight case against him."

"Then why is he roaming free?" Susan wiped her face with a paper towel.

"One of life's great mysteries. We had a court date and everything. It was a slam dunk. Then my boss comes in and says we're dropping the case. Just like that. Next thing I know the Chadwick kid walks out the door."

"Come on back," said Tim. "Now we're going to work on elbow strikes—up, down, and to the side. Keep your hands eye-level, talk to distract your attacker, then give it to him."

This is exhausting and my wrist hurts, but what a great program. When Annalise and Mia are old enough I'm bringing them to Tim. No one will attack my granddaughters. I wonder if he's got any tricks on how to fight off an angry guard dog.

Susan was paired with Lynette's friend to practice grabbing a rubber knife from an attacker. "If you had to give it your best guess, what do you think happened with Jordan Chadwick?"

"The kid had plenty of money. He could have paid off a judge, or had a connection somewhere."

"Was the DEA involved by any chance?"

"It's local unless state lines are crossed." He grabbed the fake weapon out of Susan's hand and pinned grabbed her wrists."

"Gotta pay attention," said Tim. "Remember, the bad guys are looking for soft targets so you gotta be aware at all times and look confident."

Tim taught them to kick between the shin and the knee, and to go after the eyes or the solar plexus. "You can't rely on your cell phone or even a gun. Takes too long to get'em out. You can wrap your fingers around the phone, or your keys, and use them to strike."

"Jack, do you think Jordan was still working with Richard after they both got off?"

"I wouldn't doubt it. Something Jordan said made me think those two had been working together for a while, even before Agromex came to town. I got the feeling he knew Richard back when he was in prison. I think he was the Mexican supplier."

Chapter 21

Every muscle in Susan's body ached when she opened her eyes the next morning. Half an hour of walking a couple of times a week had done nothing to prepare her for the punching and kicking she'd done last night. She popped two Aleves, jumped into the shower, and feeling slightly better after the warm water worked its magic, headed downstairs.

Audrey, wavy scissors in hand, was sorting through photos she'd spread out on the coffee table. Susan mumbled a quick 'good morning,' and went into the kitchen.

"Good morning." She gave Mike a kiss. *He's rubbing his wrist. I'm glad I'm not the only one who felt her age after last night.*

"Susan, are you really going back to that prison?" Mike packed his lunch while sipping a mug of coffee.

"I want to find out if Jordan Chadwick visited Richard. I also had another crazy thought. What if something romantic was going on between Carmella and Bruce at the same time Carmella was carrying on with Richard?"

"You mean like a little prison love triangle?"

"If Richard found out, maybe he threatened Carmella and she killed him in self-defense."

"That's grasping at straws. Does Lynette know what you're planning?"

"Yes. In fact, she's coming with me. We aren't actually going to the prison. We're going to the diner down the road from the prison where the employees eat lunch. I won't be anywhere near the prisoners. I made friends with one of the guards last time I was there. I'm hoping he'll help me out."

"Well, as long as Lynette will be there I guess you'll be safe."

"And now I have self-defense training. I'm set." She punched the air, then grabbed her still sore arm with the opposite hand.

"Something wrong with your arm?"

"I'm fine." She kissed him goodbye.

Audrey ambushed her on the way out. "Where are you going? Love triangle? Did I hear you say prison?"

"Yep. I hear Lynette's car. There are more scrapbooking supplies on the top shelf of the hall closet if you need them." She zipped her jacket. "Have fun."

Lynette unlocked the car door and Susan slid into the passenger seat. "Hey, Mom. How was the self-defense training?"

"Excellent. In fact, when the girls are old enough I want them to take it."

"I'm all for empowering girls. I've heard excellent things about the instructor."

Lynette was overprotective of her girls, much more than she and Mike had been with either her or Evan. Then again, the world was more dangerous now. Who would have imagined the number of murders that had taken place recently in their little town of Westbrook?

"You know, Lynette, I was wondering if you think Annalise is old enough to enjoy Disney World. Mike and I would love to make a trip with her over the summer. It'll be good for her to feel like she's doing something Mia is too little to do. Besides, you know how much Dad and I love spending time with her."

Lynette thought about it, then answered, "I think she's old enough. As long as Dad is there to supervise."

"Lynette!"

"Just kidding. I'll have to run it by Jason, but I think she'd love it."

"How's she enjoying preschool?"

"She loves it. They hired a Spanish teacher after Christmas."

"So that's why she said *hola* when she picked up the phone last night."

They turned off the highway at the exit for Bayersville State Correctional facility. They passed several farms spread out between thick areas of pine trees and bare apple trees. Instead of following the mountain road directly to the prison, Lynette turned on a side street. Susan assumed this was downtown Bayersville—a paint store, a rundown drugstore, a movie theater which looked like it hadn't been updated in the last century, and a classic metal diner.

"Here we are. Hope you're hungry," said Lynette. She parked in front of the diner.

"How do you know this is where we'll find the prison guard?"

"Look around. Do you see any other restaurant on this street? The next nearest lunch place is a good thirty minutes away, and they still haven't repaired the employee's lunchroom at the prison since the fire last fall. Unless the employees want to eat in their cars, this is their only option."

Susan followed her daughter into the diner and faced a long counter with red, vinyl-topped stools. An array of pies and oversized cookies under a glass cake cover caught Susan's eye. Armed with laminated menus, they slid into a booth and studied the possibilities.

"What are you getting?" She pulled out her meter and checked her blood sugar.

"Burger and fries. My favorite," said Lynette, "and a strawberry milkshake. They have salads."

I'm tired of her trying to control my diet. "Burger and fries sounds good." When the waitress came for their order, Susan added cheese and bacon, ignoring Lynette's disapproving expression.

While they waited for their food, a group of people came in.

"Lynette, that's him!" She pointed to a heavy set man with dark, wavy, slightly receding hair. Under his coat he wore a uniform. "It's Guard Jelly Belly. That's what I used to call him."

"I'd suggest you don't address him that way or he's not going to be very cooperative."

"Of course not. I never called him that to his face." She slid out of the booth and ran over to the counter where he'd just been seated. Coming up behind him, she spoke directly into his ear.

"I hear the burgers are good."

The guard jumped. Turning around, he said, "Oh, no. Don't tell me..."

"It's Susan Wiles. You remember me, right? We were locked in together when one of the prisoners went missing last year?"

The guard pushed back on the stool. "Not you again. What are you doing here? I thought once your uncle was released you'd have no reason to be back."

"I came to see *you.* I'm here with my daughter, Detective Green from the Westbrook Police." She pointed to Lynette, who waved meekly and flashed an expressionless smile.

"I only have half an hour to eat. What do you want?"

Susan pulled her phone from her pocket. "My uncle Richard was murdered Christmas Eve. I'm helping with the investigation, since its's my mother who's the number one suspect. She's my birth mother, not the one I grew up with who I consider..."

"Stop! I don't need your whole life story. Ask what you want to ask before I change my mind about talking to you."

She showed him Carmella's picture. "Do you know her?"

"Yeah. She used to come every week to teach a literacy program. Your uncle used to look forward to it. His cellmate, too."

"Did his cellmate, Bruce Feinstein, continue the literacy program after Richard was released?"

"Yeah. Like clockwork. He was trying to get his GED. Said he never graduated high school and was looking to be able to get a job when he got out."

"Did you sense anything…well…romantic going on between the two of them, or between her and my uncle?"

"I think your uncle was pretty smitten with her. Can't say whether or not the feeling was mutual."

"And Bruce? Was there any sort of, you know, jealousy there?"

The guard began to laugh. "Jealousy? Bruce played for the other team if you know what I mean. He was more attracted to Richard than he would'a been to that literacy lady."

So when I saw him and Carmella shoulder to shoulder at Barnes and Noble, she was simply tutoring him. She turned to the picture of Jordan Chadwick. "Did you ever see this man visit *Uncle* Richard?" She nearly choked calling him that, but wanted the guard to think she was motivated by a sense of family duty.

"Yeah, sure. Brought him to visit both Bruce and Richard more than a few times. He's the CEO of that Mexican company. Came to visit long before Agrowmex came to town."

"And he continued visiting afterwards?"

"Yeah. Got the feeling it was some shady business dealings. After Richard got sprung, I heard him and Bruce talking about whether or not Richard was gonna double-cross them. Something about keeping the money or something like that."

Lynette walked over to them. "Our lunch is here."

Susan thanked the guard. "If you hear anything you think might be helpful, here's my number." She started to write on a napkin, but Lynette intercepted.

"Here's my card. If you have further information to share, you can contact me at the Westbrook Police Department."

Chapter 22

As soon as she got home, Susan called Jonathan and told him about the visit.

"Susan, I haven't found any witnesses who can place Jordan at the hotel the night of the murder. In fact, we only have Audrey's word that Jordan visited Richard at the hotel at all."

"He doesn't have an alibi."

"He says he was home alone. Just because it's hard to prove doesn't mean it's not true. Besides, I'm working on something else. I went back out to the hotel and spoke to the clerk again. He says a big white guy had been hanging around the hotel. He thought he was a friend of a guest. On Christmas Eve, he showed up dressed in a repairman's uniform and told the clerk he was there to fix the vending machine on the second floor."

"So?"

"The clerk said he was surprised because normally when the machine eats money or is empty, at least half a dozen guests call to report it. I told Jackson and he called the vending company. They had no record of sending anyone out to fix a vending machine. In fact, the company was closed for the holiday."

"Big white guy. Do you suppose it was George?"

"Jackson showed him a picture, but the clerk couldn't be sure."

"I think it's time we go to Florida. I'll check the flights."

Susan spent the afternoon comparing flights and checking for reasonably priced hotels in Banyan Beach. Winter was tourist season, and rates were sky high. Using her AARP card and Jonathan's frequent flyer miles, she ultimately managed to put together an affordable trip.

Audrey came up behind her and startled her. "You and Jonathan are going to Florida?"

"Yes. We have a few things to check out for your case."

"Like what? Do you have another suspect?"

"Jonathan thinks we should interview Richard's friends down there, maybe turn up something. The trial date is closing in and we don't have another suspect."

"What about Jordan Chadwick?"

"He's our only lead. If he and Richard were in on the drugs…"

"Richard stopped doing that when he was caught at Agrowmex. He got off on that technicality and was a changed man. Said it was God giving him a second chance."

"Okay, Audrey. You had to know he was wheeling and dealing while you two lived in Florida after he got out of prison. Whatever."

Mike came in toting a grocery bag. "I stopped and picked up a rotisserie chicken and salad. Didn't know when you'd be home from the prison."

"The diner. We went to a diner in downtown Bayersville, not the prison."

"Learn anything useful?" He put the bag down on the table.

"Jordan visited Richard in jail *before* his family moved to Westbrook. Jonathan and I are flying to Banyan Beach tomorrow to look for a connection between him and Richard." *And see if my brother's story pans out. Why was he lying?*

"We don't have the money for you to go flying down to Florida on a whim. I thought we were saving to take Annalise to Disney this summer?"

"I found a good deal, but Jonathan insists on taking care of it."

"I doubt it'll be worth the money, but I guess Jonathan's getting desperate for reasonable doubt."

Susan grabbed plates and set the table. The chicken smelled delicious and she hadn't eaten since the bacon cheeseburger at lunch. Audrey caught them up on the daytime talk show topics while they ate.

"Dr. Phil had on a guy who thought his wife was trying to poison him. Mike, if you thought Susan was poisoning you, would you go to the police, or sign up for the *Dr. Phil Show*?"

"With Susan's cooking, I wouldn't want to jump to any conclusions."

Susan gave him a swat. "Lynette says Annalise is old enough to enjoy Disney. She has to run it by Jason, but she thinks it'll be fine to take Annalise on a special trip with her grandparents. Remember how my mother took Lynette down to the city to eat lunch and shop at Macy's? And Lynette still talks about how the organ came up from the floor at the Radio City Easter Show."

Audrey looked uncomfortable. Mike put down his fork.

"Of course you're thinking about your mother. Tomorrow's the anniversary of her death."

"Our flight to Florida isn't until later in the day. I thought maybe I'd pick up Annalise and bring her to the cemetery in the morning, then drop her off at school. I want to keep Mom's memory alive. We can put flowers on the grave."

"I'll come with you."

"No, you shouldn't miss work. I'll give Lynette a call and see if it's okay with her."

After dinner, Susan cleared the arrangements with Lynette and then packed for her trip. She'd hate for the girls to grow up thinking Audrey was their great grandmother. *My Mom would have eaten those two up. I bet she's sitting up there in heaven wishing she could have been alive long enough to hold them in her arms.* She wiped the tears from her eyes, then called Jonathan to finalize the travel arrangements. When she headed back downstairs, she heard Audrey whispering into her phone.

"Yeah, it's all on track. Hope they talk to a few friends and colleagues back home. It'll only strengthen my case. Gotta go." Audrey jumped when she realized Susan was standing behind her.

"Who were you talking to?"

Audrey didn't miss a beat. "George. I was telling him I hoped you'd find news about Richard's real killer when you go to Florida. This is our last hope, isn't it?"

"Audrey, you have to know more than you think you do. Richard had to have other enemies. We've explored the drug angle, the mistress angle…help me out here."

"Wait a minute. We're assuming Richard's killer is someone he recently ticked off. Maybe it's someone from the past. I mean the real past, before Richard was a changed man."

"What do you mean?"

"Richard was cleared of Maggie's murder after serving thirty years in jail. Maybe someone out there believes he was guilty after all."

"We found her real killer. It was all over the news."

"Yes, but Maggie's sister and friends were convinced Richard was guilty. I don't know, maybe they still blame him for playing a part in her death."

"After all this time?"

"Richard was in jail most of that time. He was cleared not that long ago."

"You may be on to something. Make a list. Brainstorm anyone you remotely think harbored a grudge against Richard. And while you're at it, maybe it goes back even further. Remember that girl back in college—Nina Johnson?"

"Yes, everyone was convinced he was responsible for the dorm fire that killed her, but we found the real culprit when we solved Maggie's murder."

"I know. We're brainstorming here. I'd better get to bed. Tomorrow's going to be a long day."

Chapter 23

Susan picked up Annalise the next morning. On the way to the cemetery, they had breakfast at iHop, then stopped at the florist.

"Which flowers do you like, honey?"

Annalise took her time, sniffing and fingering practically every flower in the store before coming to a decision. "I like these for your Mommy." She pointed at an arrangement of pink roses. Susan knew whatever they picked wouldn't last long outside in winter, but it was the act of commemorating her mother's death that was important.

"Okay. We'll take these." She handed the florist her ATM card. "Annalise, do you want to bring a flower to your teacher?"

Annalise jumped up and down. "Yeah, yeah. I want to give her one of these and one of these, and one of these." She pointed to three, multi-olored carnations, which Susan added to her purchase, before strapping Annalise into her booster seat and driving to the cemetery. They sang songs together as they made their way past the church, to the cemetery.

"Here we are." The iron gates of the small cemetery were propped open, and Susan followed the road to the parking area. In the warmer months, Susan made regular visits, but during the winter months, she visited less frequently. The sun struggled to make an appearance through the gray, stratus clouds. She grasped her granddaughter's hand tightly, while carrying the flowers in her other hand.

"It's right over here. See. That's your great grandmother, Emma Elizabeth Burrows. She died when you were still in your mommy's tummy. You see her name carved on the stone? You have great grandma's name as your middle name. Annalise Emma Green."

"Can she see me from heaven?"

"Yes, sweetie. And she loves and watches over you. She had so much goodness in her heart. She always knew if I was sad and she'd make me special meals like macaroni and cheese or chocolate chip pancakes."

"Just like I had for breakfast."

"Yes. And when your mommy was a little girl, her favorite place to be was at Grandma's house. Grandma spoiled your mom and your uncle Evan to pieces. She had a candy closet and first thing your mom and uncle Evan did when they got there was to climb up on the counter and eat up all the chocolate!"

"Isn't Grandma Audrey your mommy? That's what Daddy told me."

"I grew in Grandma Audrey's tummy, but when I was just a baby, I was adopted by this lady here." She patted the headstone. "She loved me so much just like your mom and dad love you and Mia." She looked at her watch. "We'd better get you to school." She laid the flowers out and kissed the headstone. Annalise did the same.

After dropping Annalise off at the Developmental Preschool, she drove over to Jonathan's. Not wanting to see Audrey immediately after visiting her real mother's grave, she'd already stashed her suitcase in the trunk. *Audrey is so different than my mom was. Mom was loving and generous, but she never would have put up with the treatment Audrey took from Richard. Mom always said you teach people how to treat you. Audrey stands up for herself with everyone, but with Richard it was different. Why didn't she put him in his place long ago? Better yet, how could she have fallen in love with him in the first place?*

She sent Jonathan a text from the driveway as soon as she pulled in and a few minutes later he slid into the passenger seat.

"How'd it go with Annalise?"

"Great. It meant a lot to me to know Mom won't be forgotten by the next generation."

"Audrey called. She said you told her to make a list of anyone else she thought may have killed Richard."

"I told her to go back to when Maggie died, and even back to when they were in boarding school and Nina Johnson died in the dorm fire."

"I did some checking. Nina had a brother who happens to live within driving distance of Banyan Beach. Audrey said he blamed Richard for the fire, even after they caught the real arsonist."

"Excellent. So we'll check him out. And we'll nose around about George and see if we can find a connection between Richard, Jordan, and drugs."

"Or simply find out just how overprotective George felt about his mother. After all, he was witness to the abuse she suffered. I've been considering that as a motive."

"Good. And meanwhile, we'll talk to some of Audrey's friends and people at the school. Want to check on our flight and see if it's on time?"

Jonathan pulled out his phone. Susan's thoughts turned to the comment Bruce Feinstein had made about Richard owing him money. And at the prison, the guard had said Jordan was worried about being double crossed. *If Richard had a stash of money, where is it? Audrey said Richard was blowing right through her retirement savings. If he had money, he'd certainly hidden it from Audrey.*

"The plane's right on time. I doubled checked our hotel reservation, too."

"It's too bad Janet couldn't tag along."

"She's saving her sick days. Wants to make a trip to visit her son in the spring. Anyway, it'll give her a chance to miss me."

"And you her! Do you see a future together?"

"I don't know. I really enjoy her company, but I feel like I'm cheating on my deceased wife. We were married for so long, I never imagined sharing my life with anyone else."

"I'm sure she'd want you to be happy. It doesn't mean you're going to forget her."

"Janet struggles with the same issue. She's been a widow for years and I'm the first person she's dated since her husband died. We're taking things slowly."

I don't think I'd survive losing Mike. It's hard to imagine ever moving on with anyone else. She looked over and saw Jonathan dozing. She turned on her audio book and drove the rest of the way to the city.

When she got nearer the airport, Jonathan woke up. "There's the sign for our terminal."

With a surge of anticipation, she pulled into the parking garage. "Florida, here we come."

Chapter 24

During the uneventful flight, Susan finished her audiobook, and Jonathan looked over his case notes. By nightfall, they were settled into a Comfort Inn in Banyan Beach, not far from Hemingway High—the private preforming arts high school which Audrey headed for decades. Exhausted by the travel, they both turned in early. Susan fell asleep immediately and when she opened her eyes, the sun was streaming through the bottom of the curtain. She quickly got herself ready for the day.

Susan walked into the hotel dining area in a pair of blue capris and a cotton shirt. She was thankful the pants still fit after the holiday pounds she hadn't yet lost.

"Good morning, Jonathan."

He put down the newspaper. "Hey, did you sleep well?"

"Like a baby." She went through the buffet line and sat down with her scrambled eggs, bagel, and fruit. Jonathan was on his second cup of coffee and had finished the *USA Today* crossword puzzle.

"I was thinking we'd start at the school. Audrey's colleagues can fill us in on her relationship with Richard. Apparently, the staff was like her family—no offense."

"None taken."

"Then, let's swing by George's work and see if we can find out how long he's been on vacation. You'll have to play the sister card."

"Got it. And I know someone here who may be a great help to us. Detective Kevin O'Hara. He's an old friend of Lynette's. We met the first time I came to Banyan Beach. Lynette gave him a heads up that we were coming and he offered to help however he can. Super nice guy."

She finished her breakfast and they walked down Franklin Street, the main drag, over to the school. By the time they got to the school, she'd taken off her sweater and tied it around her waist. She'd forgotten how beautiful the campus was with its Italian stone buildings and lush arboretum.

"This is the administration building."

Jonathan followed her inside. "Where are we going?"

"It's this way. She's retired, but they kept her office in tact, hoping she wouldn't be a stranger. From what I hear, she's still an integral part of the school."

They passed an open door and Susan peeked in. A blond, middle-aged woman sat behind a desk littered with family photos. Framed needlepoint hung on the wall above the phone.

"Susan Wiles! Audrey's daughter. We've missed you. You were quite a hit with students and faculty when you subbed for Celia Watkins, the poor, murdered choral teacher may she rest in peace. We still talk about how you and your daughter helped solve the case."

"Peggy! You look fantastic. How much weight have you lost? You look like you're fading away."

"Just about forty pounds. Finally got my act together when the doctor said I had sleep apnea and was going to have to hook up to a machine at night so I wouldn't stop breathing and die in my sleep. Scared the Bejeebees out of me. How's Audrey holding up?"

"Going a little stir crazy. You know what happened, right?"

"We heard. Poor Audrey. She's finally free of that no good mooch and they're blaming her for his murder!"

"This is Jonathan Stirling, my father and Audrey's attorney. We're trying to find info that can strengthen Audrey's defense."

Jonathan extended his hand. "Nice to meet you."

"Peggy, did you notice any change in Audrey's behavior after she married Richard?"

"Oh, yes. Your mother was always so take charge, so confident. And sharp as a tack even as she got up in years. Once she married Richard, her whole demeanor changed."

"What do you mean?"

"She became depressed and insecure much of the time. Had trouble making decisions—kept second guessing herself."

"And you think it was because of Richard?"

"No doubt. He hung around here a lot, like he didn't trust Audrey when she was away from him. Put her down constantly right in front of me, her colleagues— even in front of the students. And he was an awful flirt. Charmed every female who crossed his path—at least that's what he thought. We were all disgusted by him."

"Can you think of anyone who hated him enough to follow him to New York and kill him?"

"Not off hand. Her best friend Trudy might know more. She's been dog sitting for Wolfie since Audrey left for New York. I think I have a phone number. They worked together for many years and remained friends after Trudy retired." Peggy flipped through her old fashioned Rolodex. "Here you go."

"Thanks. I know Audrey misses you and all her friends here."

"Whatever I can do to help. We miss her, too."

Anxious to talk to Trudy, Susan and Jonathan sat down in the arboretum to make arrangments. Susan pulled out her phone and tried the number. "It's ringing."

"Trudy, I'm Susan Wiles, Audrey's..." she still choked on the words, "Audrey's daughter. I'm here with Audrey's attorney. Would you mind if we drop by and ask you a few questions? She's doing okay, considering. We'll be over shortly."

Jonathan said, "I take it we're going for a visit." They got up just as the bell rang and students crisscrossed the campus. "This feels more like a college than a high school." He followed Susan back to the hotel, where she'd left the car.

The ride to Trudy's was scenic. The sky was bright blue and cloudless, and the road was flanked with palm trees. It was certainly a mood boost after living in the midst of the gray New York winter. Trudy lived in a 55 and older condo on the beach.

"She must feel like she's on a permanent vacation," said Susan. "Imagine having the beach in your backyard. She's on the third floor."

"It's very enticing, but remember they get hurricanes down here. I wouldn't want to evacuate every time they had a warning." He pressed the elevator button.

"Audrey told me Trudy's husband was a successful doctor and left her well taken care of, contrary to Richard, who blasted through most of Audrey's savings." She rang the doorbell and immediately heard Wolfie bark.

"Susan, come on in. I assume this is Audrey's attorney." Wolfie jumped up and licked Susan's chin. "Yes, he's quite the watchdog. Loves everyone—except Richard. He growled whenever Richard came into the room."

Jonathan extended his hand. "Jonathan Stirling. Nice to meet you."

"Stirling? Like Richard?"

"They were brothers, but Jonathan is nothing like Richard."

They followed Trudy into a living room filled with dark, antique furniture. The walls were covered with tasteful oil paintings. She and Jonathan sat on the velour-covered sofa while Trudy brought out a tray with a pot of tea and delicate China cups.

"We're down here looking for alternate suspects in Richard's murder. We've come up more or less empty handed up in New York, and with the trial approaching…"

"Reasonable doubt. I see it all the time on my detective shows. You need another suspect. I'm not sure if I can help you. I will say Richard treated Audrey like dirt, and in front of him she cowered, but she's a tough cookie. When it was just the two of us, she was her old self."

"When I came down last time, drugs were a problem. Did you ever get the sense that Richard was involved in anything like that?"

"I never thought about it. He *was* a shady character. Always taking phone calls outside, not in front of Audrey. Sometimes he'd go out and not come home until the next morning. Worried Audrey sick at first, then she kind of accepted it."

Jonathan said, "Did Audrey suspect he was having an affair?"

"She mentioned that once or twice, but don't think she ever confirmed it. I miss my friend! I thought about flying up there, but then who'd watch Wolfie? I'm glad she has her other friend up there."

"Hopefully, she'll be back home really soon." *Not soon enough. I feel like I'm tripping over her wherever I turn.* "Wait. What *other* friend?"

"Someone she met when she visited Richard in New York. Coco. Coco came down here to visit a few times, though I never had the pleasure of meeting her. Liked the outlet malls, which was good for Audrey as I never was up to all that walking."

"Coco who? Did she mention a last name?"

"No, I'm sorry. I'm surprised Audrey didn't mention her. Surely they've been in touch since she's been in New York all this time."

Audrey has never mentioned having a friend in New York. Why not? She finished her tea and thanked Trudy for seeing them. As they got up to leave, Trudy said, "Did she tell you about her gun?"

Did I hear her right? "The gun? She said she bought Richard a gun because he couldn't get one being a convicted felon."

"Oh, no. She got the gun on her own. Went to the gun show at the convention center. Said it made her feel empowered."

"That's interesting. Did she know how to shoot a gun?"

"Beats me. She took some sort of online gun safety course, but that's all I know." She walked them to the elevator.

As soon as the door closed, Susan spit out, "Audrey bought a gun? She lied to us!"

"We have to do some fact checking before we jump to a conclusion. Trudy seemed a little confused, don't you think?"

"She seemed perfectly sharp to me."

"Didn't you mention meeting with Lynette's friend, the detective?"

"Yes, in fact, I'll see if we can meet for dinner."

"He'll be able to tell us if Audrey applied for a permit and if she spent any time at the shooting range. Meanwhile, didn't you want to drop by George's office?"

"Yes. Let's grab some lunch and drive over."

Chapter 25

After lunch, they drove to the Drug Enforcement Agency. George had taken Susan and Lynette on a tour when she'd first come to town to meet Audrey, and she hoped someone would remember her.

"Here we are." She pulled into a parking garage. The peach building with white shutters and a decorative roof looked more like a fancy hotel than an office building.

Jonathan pulled open the heavy glass door. "After you."

Susan looked at the wall by the elevator. The DEA shared space with a bank, a mortgage company, and a law firm. "It's on the second floor. Am I dressed okay?" She watched two women in business suits get into the elevator toting briefcases.

"You blend right in with the other retired people we've seen since we landed. It's not like you're going on a job interview." Jonathan held the elevator door for an elderly gentleman carrying a stack of manila folders. "It should be the first door on the right."

Susan followed Jonathan into the DEA office. She immediately recognized the receptionist, though she didn't remember her name.

"Can I help you?"

"I'm Susan Wiles, George Robert's sister. We met a few years ago. You were expecting a baby."

"Yes, I remember. That baby turned out to be a Tasmanian devil! Just started preschool and he keeps both me and his teacher on our toes. Gotta love it. What can I help you with?"

Although she knew the answer, she asked, "Is George working today? We're hoping to surprise him. This is my father, Jonathan Stirling."

The receptionist's expression changed. "Didn't he tell you? George hasn't worked here for months."

"I knew he was on vacation, down in the rainforest, but I thought…"

"George in the rainforest? He complained if the air conditioner was set higher than 72 degrees in here. Can't imagine that'd be his choice of a vacation spot, but nonetheless, he's gone. His back had been giving him trouble. I'll bet he got a nice disability settlement."

"You're sure?"

"Yeah. I'm surprised he didn't tell you."

"We've been out of contact lately, but I'm going to track down my brother and give him a piece of my mind for not telling me."

"Be easy on him. Some of the guys in this place would rather be caught dead than admit to succumbing to a physical injury. You know the type—macho. Anyhow, when you do find him, tell him Reina says hello."

"Thanks, Reina. And enjoy that son of yours, they grow up fast."

Did Audrey know George had retired? She'd mentioned something about him hurting his back.

When they were back in the car, Jonathan said, "What's next? We have a few hours before we meet Lynette's friend."

"How about we stop by Audrey's house. I have a key."

"For what purpose?"

"Things aren't adding up. Audrey buys a gun and has a close friend in New York we never heard about. And George retired and didn't say a word about it?"

"Let's go back and talk to Peggy at the school, too. Didn't George do some gardening work on campus? Surely she knows him."

"Yes, I forgot about that. We can do that now while Peggy's still there."

Susan turned back toward the school. When they arrived on campus, it was quiet. She remembered the schedule from when she substituted for the dead choral director. Classes were over for the day, with the exception of rehearsals. On the way to the administration building, they passed a group of students studying on the grass, and a boy practicing violin in the arboretum.

When they reached the administration building, Peggy was coming out the door.

"Hey, Susan. Forget something?"

"We just went over to the DEA office to drop in on my brother and found out he'd retired months ago. Did Audrey mention that?"

"No, but George hung around here a good deal. Hovered over his Mom like he was protecting her. Richard constantly showed up to check on what Audrey was doing, and there was George behind him. Fought like the devil, those two. One time Audrey threw them both out of the office. She was so mad. She kicked them out and slammed the door behind them. Talked about buying a security system and giving neither one of them the code."

"Has George been around lately?"

"Not for a while. Not since Audrey went up to New York. Sorry, I need to get home. We're having dinner guests."

"Have fun. Thanks for all your help." Susan and Jonathan walked back to the car. "Do you think we have time to go by Audrey's before we meet with Kevin?"

"A little," said Jonathan. "Let's take a ride."

Audrey lived close to the school. She'd told Susan she used to walk to work when the weather wasn't too hot. Susan hoped Audrey hadn't added a security system! She pulled into a neighborhood filled with white, stucco houses. If not for the black numbers nailed next to the front door, she wouldn't have been able to pick out Audrey's house.

"Come on." She turned the key, half expecting an alarm to sound. When none did, she breathed a sigh of relief. She led Jonathan across the white tile and into the living room where a beige couch housed colorful, Mexican print throw pillows. "Where do we start?"

Jonathan pointed to a roll top desk. "How about there?"

Susan rummaged through the drawers. "Appointment cards—dentist, doctor. Wait, psychologist, not doctor." She flipped over the card. "She specializes in helping victims of abuse. At least Audrey was seeking help."

"Here's a stack of bills," said Jonathan. He rifled through them. "She was two months behind on the mortgage and this credit card bill shows she's at her limit."

"Here's a postcard. I didn't think people still sent postcards. It's from Paris. *Wish you were here, Coco.*"

"So she did have a friend named Coco. She was seeking help from a psychologist, and she was behind on her bills. Open the top."

Susan lifted the top but it was locked. "Now what?"

"The key has to be nearby." He checked the drawers, then pulled them out and ran his hand across the bottoms. "Found it." He opened the desk top.

"What was so important she had to lock it away from Richard?" She pulled papers from the cubbies. "More bills. And look. One's for a premium on a life insurance policy. She had life insurance on Richard. And this bill is marked *paid.*"

"Good for her. She can cash that in—if she doesn't wind up in jail."

"And if she goes to jail, who gets the money?"

Jonathan read through the policy. "You and George get to split it. I wonder if George knew about this. It's a lot of money, even split two ways."

"She never said anything to me about it."

Jonathan continued to go through the papers. "Here's a receipt for the gun she bought. Is that her signature?"

"It sure is."

"To be fair, she did say she bought the gun for Richard."

"Then why did she feel the need to lock the receipt in here?" She pulled open a drawer in a small filing cabinet alongside the desk. "Looks like all sorts of receipts and warranties filed in here. Why not the one for the gun?"

"Who knows." He looked at his watch. "We'd better go if we want to get to the restaurant on time."

Susan put the papers back as best she could and relocked the desk. "Let's go."

Chapter 26

"Here we are. Antonio's. I wonder if Kevin's here yet."

She and Jonathan worked their way around the take-out counter which dispensed cardboard pizza boxes to a steady line of customers. The checkered table cloths and opera music playing in the background reminded Susan of Vinny's Italian restaurant back home. Conditioned like one of Pavlov's dogs, she salivated at the delicious aroma of tomato sauce, fresh bread, and hot cheese. Italian food was her hands down favorite. The tables were lit by wax-covered wine bottles masquerading as candles holders.

Shiny menus in hand, the hostess escorted them to their table.

"There's Kevin." Susan ran over and gave him a hug.

Kevin was tall and muscular with a professional looking hair style. He kissed Susan on the cheek. "How's my favorite music teacher?"

"Just fine. Are you still singing tenor when you're not busy being a detective?" She turned to Jonathan. "Kevin sang in my fifth grade choir back at Westbrook Elementary."

"Only in the church choir," said Kevin. "And I've been known to sing in the shower. How's Lynette? I heard they adopted a little girl from China."

"Yes, Mia. She's a doll."

"Daniel and I adopted a son out of the foster care system. His name's Tyler and he just turned eight last week."

"Congratulations! I'll bet you're a wonderful father. Kevin, this is *my* father, Jonathan Stirling."

"I can see the resemblance."

They ordered soft drinks and perused the menus. Susan was wavering between the mushroom ravioli and the eggplant parm, but by the time the waitress came back with their drinks she'd decided on the eggplant.

"So what can I help you with? Lynette said your mother is going to trial for killing her husband. I couldn't believe it when she told me. You must be dying of worry."

Jonathan said, "I'm trying to clear Audrey, but we we're running out of plausible suspects. Was Richard still involved in the drug trade? Possibly, but we have nothing tangible. We're hoping you can help us brainstorm."

Susan added, "He was a person of interest in an arson case which resulted in murder back when he was in school in Atlanta. They arrested the person behind it, but we hear the girl's brother still blames Richard. We're going to see him tomorrow."

Kevin said, "After Lynette contacted me, I looked at what we had on Richard Stirling down at the station. Several reports of domestic abuse, but the wife never pressed charges. We never pinned any drug charges on him either."

"Did he try to obtain a gun permit?" asked Jonathan.

"Not him, but your mother, Audrey Stirling, obtained a permit six months ago."

Susan said, "Did she have to prove she could handle a gun?"

"No, but typically new gun owners run right out to the shooting range to get some instruction. I can check on that tomorrow."

"That would be great. Do you remember my half-brother, George Roberts? He was with the DEA."

"Of course. I met him when we were investigating the Celia Watkins case at Hemingway High. He knew his stuff. Not only did he put an end to the drug onslaught at the school, he also helped clean up some local *pain clinics*. How's he doing? You should have asked him to join us."

"He's in New York with Audrey. Says he's been on vacation, but when I went by his office today, the receptionist said he took early retirement and hasn't been there for months."

"Good for him."

"But he didn't tell any of us, not me, not even Audrey."

The waitress brought the food to the table. Susan couldn't wait to dig in.

"You know how us guys are. Probably felt like retiring was a sign of weakness, especially in an active career like he had. Didn't your husband go through that?"

"No. He's cut down on his hours, but can't bring himself to retire."

"See. And not that it's any of my business, but Jonathan, you're actively trying a murder case and you're how old?"

Jonathan swirled his spaghetti against the spoon. "Touché."

They ordered coffee and Italian cheesecake for dessert. While they were finishing up, Audrey called.

"Yes, Audrey. We're at dinner with Kevin— Detective O'Hara. You remember him, right? What? You just now thought of it? Okay. We're going out to see him tomorrow. Tell Mike I'll call him when I get back to the hotel."

"Something wrong?" asked Jonathan.

"She remembers Nina Johnson's brother sent letters to Richard while he was in prison. The letters were threats, saying he was glad Richard would rot in jail because he knew even if he didn't light the fire, he was responsible for Nina's death; if he ever got out he'd have to watch his back—something like that. She wanted to make sure we talk to him." *I'll talk to her later about George retiring and her friend Coco.*

"Hopefully it's a lead," said Kevin. "Now, what have you found out since arriving here?"

"Richard was verbally abusive, and a big flirt. Audrey acted insecure and bought a gun. She had a friend we didn't know about. She owed money on her mortgage and was late on bills…"

"And," added Jonathan, "she'd taken out a life insurance policy on Richard. Kept it locked in her roll top desk."

"And you're sure she's innocent?" said Kevin.

Susan hesitated. *What kind of a daughter am I, even entertaining the thought that Audrey snapped and shot Richard?* She took a swig of water. "We're sure."

Chapter 27

"I enjoyed meeting Kevin last night," said Jonathan. Over the din of the deli, he had to repeat it in order for Susan to hear. The waitress topped off his coffee and he said, "Have you got any butter for this?" pointing to his sesame seed bagel.

"Butter?" She put her free hand on her hip.

"Yes, butter." After she walked away from the table, he said to Susan, "What's wrong with that? She looked at me like I had three heads."

"The authentic way to eat bagels is to smother them with cream cheese. They call it a smear." She dunked hers in her coffee. "I hope we find out something when we talk to Nina's brother. He lives about an hour south of here."

"I'll drive if you navigate. Did you talk to Mike last night?"

"Yes. He thinks talking to Nina's brother will be a waste of time, but Audrey thinks it will be worthwhile. It's not like we have much else, and Lynette and Jackson confirmed he'd taken a flight to New York around the time of the murder."

"George *hovered over* Audrey. Those are the words Peggy used over at the school."

"What are you saying?"

"If Lynette thought your life was in danger because Mike was abusing you, what would she do?"

"She'd find a way to throw him in jail, she wouldn't kill him." She finished the last sip of orange juice. "Are you about ready?"

Jonathan paid the bill and they hopped into the rental car looking for I-95. They'd been warned that rush hour traffic was heavy, and even after their late breakfast, the roads hadn't entirely lightened up. Susan was glad to let Jonathan drive. He was used to Atlanta traffic, while she barely ventured off the local roads back home.

She read the MapQuest directions on her phone. "We're looking for the Sawgrass Expressway." Once they got off of I-95, the traffic cleared up. Jonathan was deep in thought as he drove silently down the pancake-flat highway. "Now we want the Coral Springs exit for Atlantic Boulevard."

A while later, they drove into a gated community with a guardhouse and waited while the elderly volunteer buzzed Nina's brother and then waved them through. Jonathan parked in the driveway of a white house on a small patch of property which looked identical to Audrey's place, only smaller.

"Mr. Johnson, I'm Susan Wiles and this is my father, Jonathan Stirling."

He shook their hands. "Jonathan Stirling. I'm sure you don't remember, but we met once way back. I was visiting my big sister and tagged along to dinner with her and her friends—you were there with a pretty sorta redhead and Nina was with your brother."

"Believe it or not, I do remember. We went to that pizza shop over on Peach Tree."

"That's right. I wonder if it's still there. Haven't been back to Atlanta since I retired. Come on in."

They followed him into the living room. "Can I get you some coffee?"

"No thanks," said Jonathan. "I'm here trying to put a defense together for that girl I was with the night in the pizza shop—Audrey Stirling."

"So you married her, did you?"

"No. It's a long story. She married my brother, Richard, and now she's accused of his murder."

"Oh, yes. I followed the entire case when he was accused of killing his wife and thrown in jail. I was horrified to hear he'd gotten released after what, thirty years? And then murdered in a hotel room?"

"His wife's real killer was found. Same one responsible for setting the fire that killed your sister. Justice was done. He'll never see the light of day again."

"Yes, yes. After all those years. Had a hard time believing it wasn't Richard Stirling that committed those crimes."

A graceful, gray-haired lady came into the living room with a plate of pastries. "I'm Sandra, Chuck's wife." She sat on the sofa next to her husband. Susan grabbed a sticky bun with pecans.

"This is awkward," said Jonathan. "The reason we're here is that, like I said on the phone, Audrey Stirling is my client. She's going on trial for shooting Richard and we're grasping at straws trying to put together a defense. I was hoping you might be able to help."

"I don't know how, but if you've got questions, ask away. I can tell you he was a real SOB. Nina called my parents more than once to say he'd embarrassed her in front of friends, yelled at her...even smacked her once. None of us put it past him to set that fire."

"Did you have any contact with Richard Stirling while he was in jail? Correspondence, perhaps?"

"What, you mean like letters? No way. He was in jail. That's all I cared about."

Susan added, "And what about after he was released? Were you angry? Did you still hold him responsible?"

"I was glad they'd found out the truth...and glad Richard wound up sitting in jail for 30 years. He didn't physically kill Nina, but he sure did a number on her self-esteem. Killed her spirit, that's for sure."

"So you didn't fly up to New York over the Christmas holiday?"

Sandra spoke up. "We did fly into Kennedy a few days before Christmas, but we were up there for a funeral. My niece died in a terrible car accident. We rented a car and drove to Hartford where she lived. Helped make the arrangements. We had a solemn Christmas dinner with my sister and her family, stayed for the funeral the next morning, and came home on New Year's Day. You can check all of this."

Susan felt like a heel. "I'm sorry for your loss."

"I can't believe you thought Chuck could have gone after Richard Stirling after all these years."

"I apologize," said Jonathan. "We were just hoping to get information. In fact, Chuck, you just confirmed that Richard was abusive, even back in his school days."

Sandra excused herself, then returned several minutes later. She handed a card to Jonathan. "See, it's my niece's prayer card. Look at the date."

Jonathan said, "I'm so sorry. We'll be on our way."

Susan and Jonathan drove silently out of the development. *How embarrassing. I'm surprised they didn't kick us to the curb as soon as we implied we suspected Chuck.* Her phone rang.

"Hi, Kevin. We're just leaving Coral Springs. Really? That's a lot of hours, right? So she would have been pretty proficient? Thanks. Yes, I'll say hello to Lynette for you."

"Let me guess. Audrey spent time at the shooting range and learned how to shoot that gun of hers."

"Quite proficient. That's what Kevin said."

"You see where that leaves us? Bruce Feinstein is out, *Snookems* is out, Nina's brother…"

"Out. I know. There's still a chance it's Jordan Chadwick."

"A slim chance. I think what we're left with is your brother George. I don't know where to go with this."

"We have to find out why George was lying, and, if he and Jordan Chadwick are in business together. Remember Jordan and Bruce were owed money by Richard."

"I can't get it out of my head that George could have been protecting his mother by killing her abusive husband."

"So we get Audrey off by putting her son on the hot seat?"

"Unless you have a better idea."

Chapter 28

Home sweet home. Susan unpacked her bag and stretched out on the bed. She was about to close her eyes when she heard Audrey's voice.

"So, Susan. What did you find out in Florida? Did you talk to Nina's brother?"

I should have locked the bedroom door. She reluctantly sat up. "We did. It was a dead end. He never wrote to Richard. I don't know where you got your information."

"Richard told me. And what about how Lynette found he bought a ticket to New York right before the murder."

"Then he and his wife rented a car and drove to Hartford for a funeral. He had an alibi. By the way, I found out you bought a gun and spent some time at the shooting range. Why did you lie about it?"

Audrey looked at the floor. "I was scared of Richard and bought the gun for protection. I never intended to use it, but having it gave me peace of mind."

Susan's phone rang. "Hello, Jonathan. Everything okay? Really? Sure, I'd love to come with you. Great. Maybe we'll solve at least one mystery." She scooped Ludwig into her arms.

"What did he want?"

"Not that it's your business, but he has a lead on finding the owner of the engagement ring he found. Now, back to you. Who's Coco?"

Audrey's face turned white. "Coco?"

"Yes, Coco. Trudy told us she's a good friend and she even came to New York recently to see you."

"We met at a support group for abused spouses. I was embarrassed to tell you. Besides, she ran away from her husband and doesn't want to be found. She asked me not to tell anyone about her."

Mike came up the stairs. "Honey, I'm home." He gave her a hug. "I missed you."

"Missed you too, even though I was only gone for two days."

"Did Audrey tell you George is coming by for dinner?"

"No, but I haven't been to the grocery store and I'm too exhausted to cook."

"No worries. We told him we'd order pizza. You look tired. Why don't you catch a nap? Audrey and I will handle everything."

Thankful for the quiet, Susan closed her eyes and took a much needed cat nap. Afterwards, hoping to shed her drowsiness before George came, she jumped in the shower while Audrey and Mike ordered dinner and set the table. *Do I believe Audrey about the gun? I guess it makes sense that she wanted to protect herself. And going to a shooting range is a far cry from shooting someone point blank. Even the insurance policy kind of makes sense. Lots of people take out life insurance. I'm sure Richard had one out on her as well.* She slipped on her trusty, black yoga pants and a teal sweater, then heard Mike's voice from the bottom of the stairs.

"Susan, George is here."

"Coming."

How should I handle George? Ask him point blank why he lied about retiring, or give him time to tell us? Does Audrey know? She came downstairs and before she could made a decision, George was in front of her dressed in jeans and a flannel shirt. He hung his jacket on the coatrack.

"Susan, how was Florida?" He kissed her cheek.

"The weather was beautiful, and we got to visit with my old student, Kevin O'Hara. He's a police detective in Banyan Beach." She unconsciously emphasized the word *detective.*

"Yes, I know Kevin. He's a cracker jack detective and a nice guy." He handed Susan the bottle of wine he'd been carrying. "I couldn't show up empty handed. Where do you keep your glasses?"

While Susan got the wine glasses, the pizza was delivered. She never got sick of Italian food.

"So, George, when do you have to be back at work?" asked Susan. "Lucky you having all this time off."

"I was hoping to stay through Audrey's trial. I have lots of personal days accumulated and if I don't use them by March I lose them."

He didn't miss a beat. "We ruled out Nina Johnson's brother as a suspect."

"Really? I was hoping that would pan out. Audrey tells me the trial starts next week."

Susan looked at Audrey. "Why didn't you tell me?"

"I just found out. Jonathan called again while you were in the shower. He was surprised it was so soon. My goose is cooked. Florida turned up nothing. We're back to where we were before your trip."

George grabbed a second slice. "So is Jonathan going with the battered woman defense?"

Audrey protested. "What battered woman defense? I may have been a little beaten up, but I didn't kill my husband! We still have Jordan Chadwick for reasonable doubt."

"And *Snookems*, right?" added Mike.

George's phone rang. "I'll take this outside."

What's so private he can't talk in the same house as us? She poured another glass of wine, hoping it would leave her relaxed but not sleepy.

"Audrey, who do you think he's talking to?"

"I have no idea. I'm sure he won't be long."

George returned and finished two more slices of pizza. *He'll have to watch what he eats if he doesn't want to get a big gut. He's used to being active at work.*

When nothing but pizza bones remained in the box, Audrey asked, "Who wants to play Scrabble?"

"I do," said George.

Mike nodded. "Me too. I'll get the game." He dug it out of the hall closet.

Audrey opened the game with a seven letter word. George on the other hand, stared at the board for ten minutes, then plopped down the word *cash* when he could have spelled *cashiers* using the open *S* left by Audrey.

Discounting George, the three of them played a fierce round, with Audrey and Susan neck and neck throughout the game. In the end, Susan eked out a win.

"I had nothing but vowels the whole second half of the game," said Mike.

George responded, "And I got stuck with a Q and an X." He yawned and looked at his watch. "I'm going to take off. Thanks for dinner."

After George left, Susan said, "I'm having an ice cream craving. How about I run over to the convenience store?"

Mike and Audrey put in their acceptable choices as the selection at the convenience store was hit or miss. Susan definitely wanted ice cream but it wasn't worth driving all the way to ShopRite.

"I'll be right back."

She got into her Prius and found herself not too far behind George. *Why's he turning toward town when his hotel is the other direction?* She made a split second decision to follow him, keeping her distance in hopes he wouldn't notice he was being tailed.

She followed him into town. Most of the businesses were closed for the day, but a few restaurants and the bookstore remained open. *He's going into the Barnes and Noble. I shoulda known. Wait. Isn't that Jordan Chadwick following him?* She gave both men a chance to get seated, then slithered inside where Jordan and George were the only customers. A sole employee stood behind the register. *They keep looking at the door, like they're expecting someone.* Her heart thumped. She crept a little closer...*a few more steps and I'll be able to hear what they're saying.*

George banged his fist on the table. "Susan! What are you doing here? You shouldn't have followed me."

"Why are you meeting with Jordan Chadwick? Are you dealing drugs together? I know you quit your job at the DEA. You haven't been there for months and you lied to us."

"Susan, shush. You'll ruin everything. Go home right now and be safe," said George.

Jordan said, "Let's lock her in the car."

Susan answered, "You think I'm going to stay put in your car?" She realized she didn't bring her phone since she'd only planned to run to the corner for ice cream.

"You'll stay put in the trunk," said Jordan. "Come on." He grabbed her, but she moved her legs into a blade stance like she'd learned in the self-defense training, and gave him a fist jab right in the eyes. Noticing an exit sign, she took off out the back door, setting off the alarm. *Now what?* She ran to her car fumbling with her keys, then sped all the way home.

She fled into her house and locked the door behind her. She couldn't catch her breath.

"Susan, what happened? You look like you've seen a ghost," said Mike.

"Did they have mint chocolate chip? asked Audrey.

Susan screamed, "Are you crazy? I was almost locked in a trunk without my phone. If it hadn't been for the training Mike brought me to, I'd probably be at the bottom of the Hudson by now. And you're asking about ice cream?"

There was a loud pounding on the front door. Susan's heart stopped. "Don't answer it! Help me push the sofa in front of the door. What if he has a gun! Will bullets go through? The door is reinforced with metal and weather stripping. That means it's bullet proof, right?"

"Susan, calm down."

"Don't open it!"

"I'm just looking through the peephole. It's George, not the bogey man."

"He *is* the bogey man. Don't open it."

Audrey said, "Don't be silly. Let George in right now." She went for the door handle but Susan knocked her away. Then she heard a woman's voice.

"Mom, it's me, Lynette. It's okay. George won't hurt you. Let us in."

"No, Lynette. You don't understand. I hope you're carrying your gun."

"Let us in and I'll explain."

Mike unlocked the door.

"Mike, don't!" Her legs felt like Jell-O. *Please, God, don't let us die. Not tonight.*

Chapter 29

Lynette barged in first. "Mom, it's okay. Sit down. George isn't going to hurt you."

"But he…Jordan Chadwick…they tried to lock me in the trunk!"

"Mom, George has been working undercover for months with Jordan Chadwick. Jordan agreed to cooperate with the DEA in exchange for forgoing prison time."

"I thought he got off on a technicality? And George is retired. He lied to us."

George said, "I'm sorry I scared you, but we were supposed to meet with the leader of the entire local opioid ring at the bookstore tonight. We had to get you out of there. We were braced to arrest him after going through with tonight's deal."

"*Were* braced, past tense," said Lynette. "Mom, we've been working together with the DEA for months and you killed the whole plan. You never learn. All that work down the drain!"

Susan's thoughts felt like they were traveling through quicksand. *DEA…Jordan and George together…undercover…*

"Mom! Did you hear me? You botched a case we've been working on for months. I'm sick of you getting in the way of police business because you're too bored to enjoy retirement. Do you have anything to say?"

"I'm…I'm sorry. I thought Jordan and George…I thought they were working together and killed Richard over the money."

"What money?" asked Lynette.

"Remember when you arrested Bruce Feinstein, he said Richard owed him money for a deal? Jordan, too."

"I can assure you that neither Jordan nor George killed Richard. Now, I need to get back to my family." She slammed the door behind her.

George said, "I don't know why you were so ready to jump on me. This is the second time you pegged me for a criminal. I have to get back to the hotel and do damage control with my boss. Your interference has set us back; I can't even imagine how much. We may never nail him now. Family. What a joke!" He slammed the door behind him.

Audrey said, "He'll get over it. You know, I'm still thinking about ice cream. Mike, is the convenience store still open?"

Mike said, "I think we all need a good night's rest. Susan, what part of 'stay out of police business' don't you understand? I can't believe that Lynette and I still haven't gotten through to you. Quit jumping into dangerous situations!"

"It wasn't dangerous."

"You didn't know that. You were hysterical when you thought George was pounding on the door to come after you. I don't know how much more of this I can take. I'm going to bed."

Audrey put her hand on Susan's shoulder. "I'm sorry. If it wasn't for me, you never would have been caught up in this. I wish I could turn back the clock. I wish Richard and I never came to New York."

"Well, hindsight is always 20/20. I'm disappointed in myself. I *still* leap before I think. I thought I'd overcome that. Now I screwed up the whole operation that would have gotten drugs out of our town once and for all."

"You were trying to help me."

"And what help have I been? The only suspect left on the list for Richard's murder is Carmella, his mistress, and the evidence is, well, there isn't any."

"I'm going to bed. I didn't kill Richard. Somehow, someway, Jonathan's going to convince the jury to believe that."

Susan tossed and turned all night. She pretended to be asleep when Mike's alarm went off, and stayed in bed until she heard the front door close. Not wanting to talk to anyone, she left Janet a message saying she wouldn't be coming in today. Her phone vibrated on the nightstand.

"Hi, Jonathan. I had a really rough night. George didn't kill Richard. Neither did Jordan Chadwick. What? I guess so. I can be ready by then."

She showered and put on her Grandma jeans with a navy pullover. "Come on, Johann. Let's get some breakfast." She scooped him up and went downstairs, thankful Audrey was still asleep.

Johann and Ludwig ate while Susan scrambled an egg for herself. What now? Audrey was going to be convicted, Lynette and Mike were both angry at her, and she'd destroyed her fragile relationship with her half-brother. Jonathan was about the only one left who still wanted to see her. Unable to finish breakfast, she sat outside on the stoop and waited for Jonathan.

"Hey, aren't you freezing out there? Get in the car. I told Terry we'd be there in fifteen minutes."

"Who's Terry?"

"Remember the couple whose address we got from the guy at the jewelry store? Turns out the McHenrys have a grown son named Terry who lives with them. He was out of town the day we were there. His parents told him about our visit and he wants to meet with us."

"That's strange. Do you think he knows something about the ring?"

"That's my hope. Let's get going."

The snow had turned dirty and slushy along the roads. Susan missed the beautiful weather and green trees back in Florida. Winter in Westbrook was depressing, especially now with the trial looming.

"How was dinner with George last night?"

I hoped he wouldn't ask. "Dinner was good, it's afterwards that was terrible. I followed George to Barnes and Noble where he met with Jordan Chadwick. Turns out they were working together to bring down the head honcho of the drug business, but I blew their cover."

"Are you kidding?"

"I wish I was. Now George, Lynette, and Mike are all mad at me."

"Sounds like it was quite an evening. They'll get over it."

"I'm not so sure. I really screwed up and Lynette was as mad as I've ever seen her."

When they reached their destination, Susan said, "What's that van in their driveway? It wasn't here last time."

"It has handicapped plates." They locked up the car and followed the sidewalk. "Now this ramp makes sense." Jonathan rang the doorbell.

"Hello, I'm Terry." Terry was slightly younger than Susan and when she bent down to shake his hand, she recognized the scent of Irish Spring. He was sitting in an electric wheelchair. "Come in. My parents ran over to the mall."

Jonathan said, "I'm glad you contacted us. As you know, I found an engagement ring in my back yard and it looks like it has at least some sentimental value. I was hoping to return it to its owner." He took the ring out of his pocket.

Terry's eyes teared. "The last time I saw this ring was when my brother, Dylan, showed it to me. I can't believe how much I let him down. Probably ruined his entire life."

"What are you talking about?" said Susan.

"Dylan was head over heels in love with the girl he called his soulmate. He'd bought this ring and planned on asking her to marry him when the time was right. Then he got the letter."

Susan wanted to pull the words out of Terry's mouth more quickly. "What letter?"

"Not a letter really. It was a draft notice. He was devastated. Dylan was a peaceful guy. Didn't believe in the war."

"Did he explore his options?" said Jonathan.

"He felt like he had none. Our father was career military and loathed draft dodgers. If he fled, he knew Dad would banish him from the family. In fact, Dylan's girlfriend was involved in anti-war protests and Dad forbid her from coming onto our property. He warned Dylan to stay away from her or risk being thrown out on the street."

Susan ached for him. "Poor Dylan. He was forced to leave his girlfriend and fight for something he didn't believe in."

"At the eleventh hour, Dylan couldn't bring himself to do it. The night before he was to leave, he'd made arrangements to hitchhike to Canada. He wanted to give the ring to his girl before he left, but my father wouldn't let him near her. He asked me to relay a message. I was supposed to tell her to meet him at the park by the river at midnight. He was going to propose, and hoped she'd run away with him."

"She said no, I take it," said Susan.

"She didn't say anything. On the way to give her the message, I got t-boned by a tractor trailer. It's a miracle

I'm alive today. I was in a coma for months, lost my memory for a while, and I've been a paraplegic ever since."

Susan gasped. "Oh my God, you poor thing! And poor Dylan. His girlfriend never knew he wanted to give her the ring."

"No. I'm sure she thought he'd left her high and dry. And he thought that her absence meant she didn't want to be with him. By the time I was out of the hospital she was long gone. I had no way of tracing her."

"What about Dylan?" said Susan. "Have you spoken to him?"

"No. Dad disowned him when he found out he'd dodged the draft. I'm sure Dylan blames me for not getting Dee over there that night. He must have given up hope that she'd be there and left the ring. He hasn't been in touch, and Canada's a big country. I have no idea where he is and I know he wouldn't want anything to do with me anyhow. He doesn't know about the accident."

Jonathan said, "So you never searched for your brother?"

"No."

Susan said, "What about the girl? Did you ever try to find her?"

"No. What would I have said? I could only tell her it was my fault, that I had no idea where Dylan was, that he wanted to propose. What good would it do?"

"Do you know her name?" asked Jonathan.

"Of course. Everyone called her Dee, but her name was Della. Della Hops."

Chapter 30

"Jonathan, we have to go by the indoor flea market and find Della! All this time she was right under our noses!"

"Not so fast. What good will it do to tell her now? She'll just be heartbroken all over again, unless..."

"Unless what?"

"Unless we find Dylan and see what his circumstances are. If he's married, has kids...if's he's even alive. No one searched for him. I know they didn't have the internet and all back then, but now?"

"Where do we start? We don't know for sure he went to Canada, or if he was there and moved away years ago."

Jonathan turned into his development. "We can start with a blanket name search, filter by age...but let's use what we know. He would have had to find a job in Canada when he first arrived. He wasn't specifically trained for anything—didn't go to college."

She ran through the conversations they'd had both with Dylan's parents and with his brother. *If you went to another country with no particular skills or training, where would you find work? He hitchhiked, so if he didn't have a car, he probably didn't venture much north of the border. Evan said there were pockets of draft dodger communities in Canada—he read it in one of those books at Barnes and Noble...*

She turned to Jonathan, "Hey, remember the beautiful ashtray? The one his mother said he made? She said he had a glass blowing hobby—she packed up his tools and they're still in the garage. She said he was starting to have success selling. We could see if he belongs to any trade associations."

"If he kept it up. Also, he was in good shape. I suppose he could have gotten work on a farm or maybe construction. I'm just brainstorming. Anyhow, we've got more pressing issues, like Audrey's trial." He pulled into his driveway. "Are you coming in?"

She followed him into the dark house and immediately noticed the flashing message indicator on his home phone. *He still has a message machine? We don't even have a land line anymore.*

Jonathan hit the button. *This call is to inform you that Audrey Stirling's trial has been rescheduled. Jury selection will begin tomorrow at 9am.*

"Tomorrow? How can they do that! Are you ready?"

Jonathan sighed. "Doesn't seem to be a choice. It's now or never. I'm going to try to pin reasonable doubt on Carmella. I don't know what else to do at this point. Let's pray for a sympathetic field from which to choose the jury."

"How can I help?"

"Help Audrey put together a wardrobe for court. Nothing too severe—go for pastels or floral prints. We want her to look soft."

"Should I get someone to come to the house and do her hair? Her roots are long overdue."

"No, leave the gray. And not too much makeup. We want the jury to see her as a victim—a victim too traumatized to have planned a murder. I have to get started. Let me drop you back home."

When Susan got home, the TV was on and Audrey was working on her scrapbooking. "Audrey, Jonathan is going to call you. The trial's been moved up. Jury selection starts tomorrow."

Audrey put down the wavy scissors. "Are you kidding? Just last night we lost Jordan Chadwick as a possible suspect. What are we going to do?"

"He's pinning his hopes on *Snookems*. Her church alibi wasn't verified, and the taxi driver says he may have driven her to the hotel on Christmas Eve."

Audrey shook her head. "I don't think...I was hoping Jonathan could come up with something better."

"Really? He's working his tail off, *pro bono,* mind you. He didn't have to step up at all. I doubt you could have found another defense attorney to even touch this case. Try being grateful."

"Okay, okay. I'm nervous and stressed as you can imagine."

Breaking news interrupted the TV program. "Susan, look!"

"It's showing an arrest. It's the drug dealer who George and Jordan were trying to help capture. Turn it up!"

"They got him! You didn't mess up the case after all."

What an incredible relief. "No, I guess I didn't. Lynette really overreacted, don't you think? Mike, too. They owe me an apology, both of them. Moving on, Jonathan said to help you pick out clothes for the trial. Do you have anything with you that might work? Jonathan says to go for a soft look."

"Honestly, I didn't pack anything appropriate for court."

"How about if I run out and pick up a few things? We can return what you don't like."

"Thanks, that would be helpful."

Susan was on the way to the mall when she had another idea. She headed downtown to Carmella's dress shop. *What do I hope to find there besides clothes for the trial?* She resisted the urge to call Lynette and seek forgiveness now that they'd arrested the dealer they were after. After she got home she planned to do some research on locating Dylan McHenry.

The shop bell jingled and Carmella instantly greeted her. "What can I help you with?"

"I need to pick up something appropriate for court. Not for me, for my mother. Something that will make her appear soft and vulnerable." *Will she realize it's Audrey who'll be wearing it when she goes on trial for murdering Richard? Have I said too much?* "Size eight, I think. If it doesn't fit, I can return it, right?"

"As long as the tags are on and you have the receipt. It's too bad you didn't bring her along." Carmella led her to a rack near the fitting rooms where she rifled through the dresses. "Here's a sweet, pink number. The Peter Pan collar and the pastel color scream feminine. And here's a navy blue A-line, simple and serious. It can be dressed up or down."

"Okay. What about this one?" She held up a floral print.

"It's pretty, but I think it'd be more appropriate for church than court."

Susan pounced on the opportunity to segue. "Yes, it's similar to something I wear to church. Some of the young ones come in with dresses that look more appropriate for a night club. Do you know what I'm talking about?"

"Yes and no. Most of the younger set at my church show up in jeans, unless, of course, it's a major holiday."

"Don't get me started. Last Christmas we went to Midnight Mass and you'd think it was more about the fashion than the Bible. Girls in this town. Do you know what I mean?"

"I went to Midnight Mass at St. Patrick's Cathedral this year. Always wanted to do that and my sister agreed to make a road trip. Beautiful service. Everyone I noticed was dressed appropriately." She grabbed a skirt suit from the rack. "What about this? It's a suit, but the fabric is soft and unstructured."

"I'll take it. In fact, I'll take all these if you don't mind, and bring back what she can't use."

"Okay, no problem." She rang up the purchases. "And here's a coupon for next time. Thank you for shopping with us."

St. Patrick's in the city! No wonder no one saw her at her own church that night. She has an alibi after all! Of course, Lynette will have to verify it. Now what? She was the last hope for reasonable doubt. She decided to stop at the police station on her way home. When she arrived, Lynette was going through a folder at the counter.

"Lynette, I have to tell you something."

"Mom, I really am not in the mood to talk to you right now." Her lips were drawn tight at the corners, her jaws barely opening when she spoke. She continued staring into the folder.

"I'm sorry about last night, but you wound up getting your suspect, right?"

Lynette looked up. "I'm really busy."

"You have to check something out. I was over at the dress shop picking up outfits for Audrey to wear to court, and guess what? Carmella and I got to talking about appropriate church attire. I picked out this floral dress for Audrey and...anyhow, Carmella was at Midnight Mass the night of the murder, but not here in Westbrook. She was at St. Patrick's down in the city! You can verify that, right? Security cameras? Toll snapshots?"

"I'll look into it."

"You have to hurry. Jury selection starts tomorrow."

Lynette glared at her. "Goodbye, Mom. And by the way, I'm reconsidering letting Annalise go to Disney over the summer with you and Dad. I can't trust you to keep my daughter safe."

"That's ridiculous! Besides, Dad will be there." *Why did I say that? Of course I'd keep her safe.*

"Bye, Mom." Lynette tucked the folder under her arm and went into her office.

I know she heard me, and she has to know what a game changer this is if it checks out.

When Susan got home, Audrey was pacing across the floor, wringing her hands together.

"What's wrong?"

Audrey took a breath after every word. "Susan, I can't calm down. I think I'm having an anxiety attack."

"You're okay. Anyone in your shoes would be feeling anxious. Take a few deep breaths." She went into the kitchen and brought back a glass of water. "Drink this. Look what I got for you to try on." She pulled the dresses and suit from the shopping bag.

Audrey took a few sips of water and her breathing calmed down. "These are beautiful. I'll go try them on."

While Audrey changed, Susan opened her laptop. *Dylan McHenry. There are hundreds here. Glass blowing shops, Canada. I can't focus.*

"How's this look?" said Audrey. She was wearing the pink dress with the Peter Pan collar.

"It's fits you perfectly. That one's a keeper. Go try the others." Audrey climbed the stairs.

Susan heard Mike's key in the door. "Oh, good. You're home early." She went to kiss him, but he brushed her away.

"You're still mad, I know. They caught the drug dealer. They said on the news they've been after him for years."

Mike grumbled, then went into the kitchen. Susan followed him. "Jury selection starts tomorrow. It looks like *Snookems's* alibi might check out after all. Jonathan must be beside himself."

"That's not your problem, it's Jonathan's. Not that it matters what I say. I'm hungry, what do we have for dinner?"

"I'll take care of it." She opened the fridge.

Susan broiled three chicken breasts and cooked a bag of instant rice. Audrey tried on the other outfits, then came down and tossed together a salad. Dinner was strained, with Mike still angry, and Audrey nervous about the trial. Susan stared at her phone, hoping Lynette would get back to her. Instead, Jonathan called and asked if he could stop over. His voice was grave and deliberate.

"That was Jonathan. He's on his way. Says he has something important to discuss with us."

"I'll clear the table," said Mike.

Jonathan arrived with grim news. "Lynette checked the security cameras at St. Patrick's. Carmella was there, just like she said. Given the time frame, she couldn't possibly have been at the hotel killing Richard. And another thing. The taxi driver who you talked to, Susan? He told you it might not have been Audrey he drove to the hotel the second time, then he remembered the scarf. He said the woman had a silky scarf with Chinese writing on it. The same woman in the same scarf was in his cab twice that night. It was you, Audrey, not *Snookems*. You came back to the hotel that night, not just the next day like you told us."

"Audrey, if what he's saying is true…"

"As your lawyer, I have to know. Carmella was our last shot at reasonable doubt."

"Audrey, think hard. Is there anything else, anything at all you still haven't told us?"

"I only have a few hours to rework this case, Audrey. Maybe he pushed you too hard that night. Was it an accident? Was it self-defense?"

"It's now or never, Audrey. You tell us the truth and let Jonathan come up with a hail Mary, or you rot in jail for the rest of your life."

Audrey froze. The silence was as wide as the Grand Canyon. "Okay... I did kill Richard!" Audrey wept into her hands.

Susan's jaw dropped. "Audrey, why?"

"I couldn't take it anymore. I snapped. He was going to kill me. I confronted him about *Snookems* and he grabbed the gun from the nightstand. He pointed it right ;at me. I don't know what came over me; it was like a rush of adrenaline. I lunged at him, grabbed the gun, and I shot him."

Chapter 31

"All Rise."

Susan, Mike, and Lynette were seated in the front row of the courtroom just behind Jonathan and Audrey. The courtroom was smaller than Susan had imagined from what she'd seen on TV shows. She looked at the jury box—mostly women, two men. The judge was an older man with graying hair and Harry Potter glasses. Audrey sat motionless, hands clasped tightly together, staring blankly at the bench.

The vibrant female prosecutor stood up, commanding the room with her confidence.

"On the evening of December 24, Christmas Eve, the defendant, Audrey Stirling, read her husband's texts, without his permission, and discovered he was having an affair. She confronted him; they argued. In a fit of rage, she took a taxi to a bed and breakfast down the road, then returned later that night with a gun and shot him in the heart. The defense will try to tell you that Audrey Stirling was the victim—that her husband deserved to die, shot dead in his hotel room, on Christmas Eve."

The prosecutor argued that Audrey had family—a support system—and had other choices rather than murder.

"This wasn't a heat of the moment decision, but rather a premeditated, cold-blooded, homicide. Audrey Stirling purchased a gun, clocked numerous hours at the shooting range, and brought that weapon with her to

New York with the sole purpose of killing her husband."

Audrey's goose is cooked. Jonathan's a good attorney, but this woman is a lioness aiming for the jugular. The jury hung on every word she said, followed her with their eyes, didn't fidget, shook their heads in agreement and the trial has barely started.

Now it was Jonathan's turn to deliver his opening statement. He rose from the table, taking confident and deliberate strides, pausing in front of the jury.

"We are here not to determine if my Audrey Stirling murdered Richard Stirling. She admits to shooting him in the chest and killing him. You the jury must determine whether or not the relentless verbal and physical abuse inflicted by Richard Stirling left a suffering wife no choice but to defend herself. My client's self-esteem had been beaten to a pulp time after time. She believed with every fiber of her being that her husband was going to kill her."

He walked to the end of the jury box. "Since the 1970's, the court has upheld battered woman syndrome as a defense in half a dozen high profile murder cases. The defense will show that Audrey Stirling suffered intense psychological abuse and did what she had to do to escape her tormentor. It was a matter of kill or be killed. You will come to understand that the defendant, an elderly, frail woman, an educator who devoted her entire career to nurturing hearts and developing young minds, should be acquitted."

Okay, Jonathan. You made a compelling point. Let's hope the jury agrees. She looked at Audrey, hands clenched, feet flat on the ground, legs trembling enough to be noticeable. She whispered to Lynette, "How did he do?"

"He clearly set the groundwork. We have to hope our witnesses can convince the jury."

The prosecutor called a psychologist to the stand who specialized in working with battered spouses.

"Have you ever successfully treated a victim of spousal abuse?"

"Many times. With therapy, a victim can learn to cope with his or her situation in a productive manner. Often it means reframing the situation—helping the victim understand that the fault lies with the perpetrator."

"Can you describe a positive outcome in any of the cases you've treated where the victim has suffered abuse equal to that suffered by the defendant?"

Jonathan jumped up. "Objection! Determining the degree of abuse suffered by my client calls for speculation."

"Sustained."

"Let me rephrase," said the prosecutor. "Have you ever had a client walk into your office and express a desire to kill their abusive spouse?"

"All the time."

"And how many of your patients wound up murdering their spouses?"

"Objection!"

"Let me rephrase. Can you give an example of a successful outcome regarding spousal abuse?"

"I can give many examples. The goal of therapy is to rebuild self-esteem and get the patient to a place where they can see the situation clearly and evaluate their options."

"What are some examples of options—other than murder."

"Objection!"

The prosecutor withdrew the comment, but the damage had already been done. The jury once again had the opportunity to hear the *M* word.

The prosecutor resumed. "What are some positive choices an abuse victim can make?"

"Couples therapy has worked in some cases. If the situation is too far gone or dangerous, the goal is to get the victim away from the abuser. We alert law enforcement if the situation is severe and/or set the victim up in a shelter or in another safe environment. Separating from the abuser and regaining control over one's life is our goal."

The prosecutor called a psychiatrist to the stand and elicited much the same responses. In the coming days, she called the owner of the shooting range who she'd flown in from Florida, the taxi driver, who said Audrey did not appear out of control the night he drove her to the bed and breakfast and then back to the hotel, and hotel employees who testified that Audrey and Richard appeared to be getting along just fine. When the prosecution rested its case, Susan was sure Audrey would be spending the rest of her life in jail.

Back at Susan's, Audrey said, "I feel completely defeated. I could have gone for therapy. I should have left Richard…"

Susan tried to reassure her. "It's part of being an abuse victim. You don't think clearly. Tomorrow Jonathan starts telling your side and you'll feel better."

At 3 a.m., wide awake, she heard Audrey go downstairs. *Should I go down and see if she's okay, or try to go back to sleep?* Knowing it'd be an uphill battle to get back to sleep, she put on her slippers and, careful not to wake Mike, padded down the steps. She was surprised to hear Audrey's voice, assuming she was on the phone.

"I don't know. So far it's been the prosecutor's turn. Jonathan chipped at the psychologist's credibility in the cross examination but I don't know if it was enough. It's safe, right? I know, that part is believable. Talk to you soon."

Susan wondered if Audrey was talking to her friend Coco, the one she'd met at the support group. She hesitated at the bottom of the steps, then decided to go back to bed, knowing Audrey had another shoulder to cry on. Morning would be here all too soon.

Chapter 32

"All rise."

Susan felt like she'd been run over by a truck. Gone were the days she could survive on a few hours' sleep. Sandwiched between George and Mike, she was thankful for the strength surrounding her. Mike had gotten over being angry, and since they'd nabbed the drug king, George no longer blamed her for messing up the undercover mission. Audrey, in the floral 'church dress' leaning on the table for support, looked the part of a battered wife.

Jonathan called his first witness, the coordinator of a women's shelter, who'd won awards for her work.

"Ms. Harper, you've worked with abused women for nearly twenty years, correct?"

"Yes, I have."

"When the women enter the shelter, what is their typical mental state?"

"They come in afraid, distraught, beaten down emotionally, worried about whether or not their abuser is going to come after them. If they have children, they fear for them."

The prosecutor jumped up. "Objection. Calls for speculation."

Jonathan rephrased. "In your expert opinion after nearly two decades of experience working with women facing similar challenges to my client's, do victims typically seek help the first time their partner hits them or verbally abuses them?"

"No, generally they suffer a long time before having the courage to come to us. Statistics support that. It's the last straw."

"What do you mean by last straw?"

"When they come to us, the victim is often at the point where she is either going to kill herself, or kill the abuser."

"So in shooting her abusive husband, Audrey Stirling was reacting in a manner you've seen from victims you've dealt with over the past two decades."

"Absolutely."

"Have any of the women you've had in your shelter gone through therapy or marriage counseling?"

"Some have."

"But yet they wind up in your shelter, even though they may have sought other types of help."

"Yes."

Next, Jonathan called Trudy Jenkins to the stand.

"Ms. Jenkins, what is your relationship to the defendant?"

"We have been close friends for many years."

"Did you notice a change in Audrey Stirling after she became involved with and married Richard Stirling?"

"Oh, yes. Audrey was always so self-confident, a real go-getter, like the energizer bunny. That's what I used to call her." She smiled at Audrey. "When Richard was in jail and faced the possibility of being released, Audrey was obsessed with proving him innocent. You know, you were Richard's lawyer back then."

"Just answer my questions, please. How did Audrey Stirling's behavior change after he was released?"

"He treated her terribly, always putting her down in front of people. She was too fat; she was getting senile—stuff like that. She seemed tired, depressed. I couldn't believe she didn't fight back—defend herself when he started in on her. She was scared of him. That's why she bought the gun."

"Did she buy a gun for the purpose of killing her husband?"

The prosecutor shouted, "Objection! Calls for speculation."

"Sustained."

"Did she share with you why she felt the need to purchase a gun?"

"She was scared he was going to go too far. Those are the words she used."

"Did she elaborate on what she meant by going too far?"

"She thought he was going to kill her one day."

After she stepped down, Jonathan called an emergency room doctor to the stand. He had treated Audrey on several occasions back in Florida and testified to the fact that the injuries she'd sustained were not likely to have been caused by simple falls or accidents. In his opinion, the injuries were indicative of abuse.

Before resting his case the next day, Jonathan called two more witnesses to the stand. One was a woman who was acquitted after using battered woman syndrome as a defense. She'd killed her boyfriend after he threw acid in her face and held a knife to her throat. She now held a degree in social work and specialized in helping abuse victims.

The second witness was a forensic psychiatrist who testified that with certain personality disorders, such as the one from which he thought Richard suffered, no amount of support or psychological help could have fixed the problem. He stated that Audrey would have wound up dead if she'd stayed with Richard.

After a late lunch, court resumed with closing arguments.

"Richard Stirling was not a stellar husband," said the prosecutor. "He had an affair, he talked down to his wife, was even known to physically harm her to the point she needed medical care. Did he deserve to be jailed for the abuse he inflicted? Possibly. Did he deserve to be murdered in cold blood? Absolutely not. Audrey Stirling is an educated woman with family and close friends living near her for support. She had the choice to seek therapy, or to divorce Richard. She could have simply moved away. Did she choose any of those options? No. Instead, she registered for a gun permit, bought a gun, practiced shooting it, and with calculated planning, murdered her unsuspecting husband." The room was silent.

Jonathan stood up and slowly walked over to the jury.

"Audrey Stirling was a giving and vital member of society—a school administrator, a caring mother, a supportive friend—until she became involved with Richard Stirling. He changed her, stripping her self-esteem, leaving her insecure and fearful of her life.

The prosecutor argues that Audrey Stirling had other choices—therapy, running away to a shelter—but you heard expert testimony refuting these options as surefire solutions. The emotional stress Richard Stirling inflicted on his wife obscured her judgement and, seeing no escape, she stopped the threat.

The defendant was prey hunted by a predator who threatened her very existence. Emotionally imprisoned by her mentally-ill husband, she suffered unduly at his hands. She poses no threat to society. Allow her to live out her remaining years with her friends and family, making positive contributions to society as she's done her whole life. Don't send her to another prison. Battered Woman Syndrome Defense is not new or frivolous. During the past fifty years there have been documented cases similar to this one where juries have chosen to acquit the victim based on it. I ask that you do the same for my client, Audrey Stirling."

Chapter 33

Susan's stomach was so upset she couldn't finish her oatmeal. Audrey stared out the window, still in her robe.

Mike looked up from the newspaper. "By this time tomorrow, I'll bet you'll be able to go outside and take a walk, or head to the mall. Jonathan gave a persuasive closing argument. The jury has to acquit you."

"Audrey, you should eat something," said Susan.

"Why? Because every meal after this for the rest of my life will be served out of the prison cafeteria?" She took a breath. "I'm sorry. I'm a bundle of nerves."

Susan fiddled with the dishwasher and poured water for the cats. "You should get in the shower. We can't be late."

Audrey sauntered up the stairs. When she was out of earshot, Susan said, "Mike, do you think she really will be acquitted?"

"I don't have a crystal ball, but the jury is mostly women and I don't think they took well to that overly aggressive prosecutor. How could they not sympathize with an old lady who was beaten down by a jerk of a husband? I'll bet they secretly admire Audrey for having the guts to put an end to him."

"From your mouth to God's ears. Audrey won't last in prison. If she's found guilty, that'll be the end of her."

Audrey, hair still damp from the shower, grabbed a glass of water. "Do I look okay? This may be the last time I ever wear street clothes. Susan, if I wind up in prison, you can take what clothes you could use and donate the rest to the woman's shelter here in town. Back in Florida, I have a pretty champagne-colored dress in the back of my closet. I want to be buried in it—when the time comes."

"Stop feeling sorry for yourself. You'll be back home with your clothes and Wolfie by this time next week."

"I hope Trudy won't mind keeping Wolfie for me if it becomes necessary. Otherwise, George may be able to take him."

Mike said, "Let's get going. Lynette texted and she's on the way to the courthouse now. George said last night that he'd meet us there."

The drive to the courthouse felt like a march to the gallows. No one spoke. Audrey stared out the car window the whole time. Mike clutched the steering wheel so hard Susan could see the veins in his hands pop out. Appropriately, the sky was gray with low hanging clouds. The weatherman predicted two to four inches of snow before the day was through.

Mike pulled into the parking garage. "Let's get this over with."

Lynette and George were already seated in the courtroom. Audrey found Jonathan, who grabbed her around the shoulder in a supportive manner. Susan knew he was at least as nervous as the rest of them. It had been a while since Jonathan had handled a criminal trial and although she was extremely impressed, she knew he would never forgive himself if Audrey wound up in prison.

"All rise."

Susan's heart pounded as the jury foreman stood up.

The judge's voice echoed in the silent courtroom. "Does the jury have a verdict?"

"Yes, your honor. On all charges of murder, we find the defendant, Audrey Stirling, not guilty."

Susan had to restrain herself from jumping up and down and applauding. Audrey collapsed into Jonathan's arms, looking too shaky to stand on her own.

"Mom, he did it. Jonathan got her off!"

George hugged them. "Thank God. I can't wait to get her back home and for all of us to resume our blissfully normal lives. Susan, your father did a fantastic job. He's going to be in demand now, you know."

"He claims to be retired, but I guess we'll see."

Audrey and Jonathan worked their way over. "Audrey, does that mean I can't have that soft velour sweat suit of yours now?"

Audrey managed a weak smile. "Tell you what. I'll leave it with you and when I come to visit I'll borrow it back."

Visit but not live with. She could handle that.

Mike said, "How about everyone comes over to the house for a celebration dinner?"

Audrey said, "I have a better idea. I want to go out! No offense, but the walls were really starting to cave in on me."

Chapter 34

Vinny's had a table set up and waiting. Vinny himself had ordered a large centerpiece for the table with a congratulations card tucked inside.

"What beautiful flowers! You have some thoughtful people in this town," said Audrey.

Mia was sitting in a highchair, and Annalise was perched in a booster seat next to Audrey. "I'm going to miss my great granddaughters!"

Susan looked at Lynette, *I hope she didn't mean what she said the other day about not trusting me.* "Mike and I are bringing Annalise to Disney this summer. Maybe we can spend a few days in Banyan Beach." *She's not objecting...*

"That would be wonderful! A new children's museum opened up last year."

"And here's to the super star defense attorney," said George. He raised a glass. "I can't thank you enough for what you did for my mother."

Jason said, "So are you going to come out of retirement, Jonathan? I'll bet after this you'll be bored now."

"I've got plenty to keep me busy." Janet sat beside him and he clutched her hand. "Oh, and I forgot to tell you—I have a lead on our mysterious ring dropper!"

"You're kidding! Did you find him?" said Susan.

"I tracked down a Dylan McHenry through the Canadian Glass Blowers' Society. I spoke to him on the phone and we're both nearly certain it's his ring. He still lives in Canada, just over the border, and he's driving down here. We can meet with him tomorrow if all goes according to schedule."

"That's amazing. How romantic, finding an engagement ring after all this time. Maybe his love is still here waiting!"

"Don't know, but I sensed he was hoping. Says he was widowed last year. I think that's why he agreed to come here so quickly."

Susan hadn't felt so relaxed since before the night Audrey called to say she'd been arrested. Not only was she happy that Audrey had been acquitted, she was looking forward to having their house back.

They feasted on Italian food, family style, topped off with spumoni and cappuccinos. Lynette took out her phone and took pictures from every angle, which she promised to share.

Mia squirmed in her highchair, a pile of spaghetti on the tray and on the floor. Susan fed her spumoni, which kept her happy for a while.

Lynette said, "We have to get the girls home and Jason and I have work tomorrow."

"Speaking of work," said Janet, "it's getting to be my bedtime. Am I getting my number one volunteer back?"

"Soon, I promise."

After extended hugs and kisses, they all headed home. Exhausted, Susan watched a bit of TV, then fell into bed next to Mike, who was already snoring.

When she woke up in the morning, Audrey was already up, dressed in a jogging suit and sneakers.

"I made myself some oatmeal and now I'm going to do something I haven't done since Christmas. I'm going for a walk. Outside. Want to come?"

"No, I got a text from Jonathan. Dylan Henry arrived ahead of schedule. We're meeting him for an early lunch. Have fun. There's an extra house key on the table by the door."

Susan drove downtown to the café where they'd agreed to meet. Jonathan was waiting for her.

"Is Dylan here yet?"

"No, but that may be him coming in now."

Dylan McHenry was thin, with silver hair and a neatly trimmed beard. He wore a plaid, lumberjack jacket, and when he removed his gloves and extended his hand, Susan noticed how delicate yet masculine it was. *Artistic hands on a man who turns glass into artwork. That makes sense.*

They sat near the window. Jonathan pulled the ring out of his pocket. "Do you remember this?"

Dylan's eyes teared up when he took it from Jonathan and read the inscription. "I never imagined I'd see it again. Della didn't show up that night. I waited as long as I could. I was heartbroken that she hadn't responded to the message I sent through my brother."

Susan said, "We met your brother Terry, and your parents, too. Terry was in a car accident that night and was in a coma for months. He's in a wheelchair to this day. Della never got the message."

Dylan's face lost all color. "Terry? In a wheelchair? Della didn't know? She must have thought I left without saying goodbye—that I abandoned her."

Jonathan said, "Why didn't you come back here after Jimmy Carter issued amnesty back in the seventies? You never even called your family, or tried to contact Della?"

"I knew my Dad had disowned me when he found out I dodged my patriotic duty. Mom would have come around, but it would have caused another World War in their house."

"But they were your parents," said Susan. "And what about your brother? Didn't you want to see him?"

"I thought Terry had blown me off and I blamed him for Della not showing up. As time went on, I wondered if she had gotten the message and decided she'd be better off without me. I never stopped thinking about her, even after I met my wife. Don't get me wrong, Claire and I had a wonderful marriage and I miss her dearly. It's just, you know, you never forget your first love."

"Maybe it's not too late," said Susan. "Jonathan found you, and we know how to find Della."

Dylan leaned in, "You know her! Does she still live here in town? Is she married?"

Susan said, "Yes to the first question, no to the second. We'll take you to her after we finish lunch."

Chapter 35

Susan couldn't wait to tell Mike and Audrey what had happened. She tossed her keys on the hall table and told them to sit down.

"After lunch, we drove Dylan to the indoor flea market. He was so nervous he was shaking. We walked him over to Della's booth and she recognized him right away. She started to cry."

Audrey said, "I'll bet she was so happy to see him. Did he propose on the spot?"

"Once she got over the shock, she was angry. Started hitting him, not like Richard or anything, just enough to make her point. She told him what a creep he was for sneaking away like that and how her heart was broken and she never trusted a man after that."

Mike said, "Good for her not putting up with his bull."

"No, there was a big mix-up. She never got the message to meet him."

"So will they live happily ever after?" said Audrey.

"It's too soon to tell, but I think it was karma, Jonathan finding the ring and getting Dylan back here. I'm rooting for a happy ending."

Mike said, "If it's meant to be, it'll happen."

Susan's phone vibrated. "It's my doctor's office." She went into the kitchen to talk. "Really? That's good, right? Thanks."

"Well? Are you dying?" said Mike.

"Nope. My A1C is down and I don't need to go on medication at this point. I can't tell you how relieved I am."

"I'm glad you squeezed in the bloodwork, even after you missed your appointment."

"Wonderful. And with the stress of the trial behind us, it'll be even easier for you to focus on your health," said Audrey. "You know, I think I'll go for another walk, myself."

After Audrey left, Susan checked her phone for the Weight Watchers' schedule. "Mike, would you mind if I go to a meeting tonight?"

"Not at all. Have fun."

Susan changed out of her heavy jeans, and drove to the Barnes and Noble. She considered it a perk that the meeting was in the back room of the bookstore and on weeks when she lost weight, she treated herself to a new book. She had just walked in when through the glass door, she noticed a taxi pull in across the street.

What on earth is she doing down here? She said she was going for a walk. If she wanted to come downtown, why didn't she ask to borrow one of our cars? She stared at Audrey through the glass, then watched her go into the cafe where she and Jonathan had met Dylan.

She looked at her watch. The meeting was about to start. Weighing her priorities, she made a flash decision. *There's another meeting tomorrow night.*

She crossed the street and peeked inside the crowded dining area. She saw Audrey sitting at a booth in the corner. *Who's she eating with?* Her companion's back was to her.

Pulling her hat over her hair and hiding her mouth with her scarf, she sat at the booth behind them. Slyly, she stole a look behind the greenery which separated her seat from Audrey's.

Oh my God, why is she talking to her? I thought they didn't know each other. She was stunned to see it was Carmella sitting across from Audrey. Susan sank into the seat to further avoid being seen and listened with every cell in her body.

"We did it!" said Carmella. "I can't believe we pulled it off."

"Piece of cake. Battered woman syndrome, my foot. You know I got that from a Farah Fawcett movie I saw on Lifetime. I think I was every bit the actress she was, God rest her soul."

"I'm so glad we met at the prison when Richard was there. Once he was released and I found out what a creep he was, I knew who to call."

"So now you get the insurance money too, right? That slimeball Richard got what was coming to him all right. Cheating on you, selling drugs to my niece and costing her her life, playing me for a fool…We girls gotta stick together. And now, the treasure."

What is she showing her? I can't turn around now.

"Half for you and half for me. I kept it hidden in the safe at the boutique this whole time after you stole it out of Richard's bag. None for Jordan Chadwick, none for Bruce Feinstein, and none for Richard. This drug money will allow me to open another shop in the next town."

"And I'll have a worry free retirement. Maybe I'll take my granddaughters on one of those Disney cruises."

Susan couldn't believe her ears. Richard's death was, in fact, planned, calculated. *Audrey has gotten away with murder in the first degree and thanks to double jeopardy can't be retried! I should have known when Audrey slipped and called 'Snookems' Carmella. And Carmella must be the friend, Coco, who Trudy told her about.*

Audrey said, "To us. To making the world a better place, my friend."

Carmella answered, "To girl power. Bon Appetite."

THE END

ABOUT THE AUTHOR

 Diane Weiner is a veteran public school teacher and mother of four children. She has enjoyed reading for as long as she can remember. She has fond memories of reading Nancy Drew and Mary Higgins Clark on snowy weekend afternoons in upstate New York and yearned to write books that would bring that kind of enjoyment to her readers. Being an animal lover, she is a vegetarian and shares her home with two adorable cats. In her free time, she enjoys running, attending community theater productions, and spending time with her family (especially going to the mall with her teenage daughter and getting Dairy Queen afterwards).

Visit dianeweinerauthor.com to find out more about the author.